THE OUTWARD ROOM

MILLEN BRAND (1906–1980) was born in Jersey City, New
Jersey, into a working-class family and was of Pennsylvania
German descent on his mother's side. Following graduation from
Columbia University in 1929, he worked briefly as a psychiatric
aide and for several years as a copywriter for the New York
Telephone Company before taking up faculty posts at the
University of New Hampshire and New York University. *The
Outward Room*, Brand's first and most acclaimed novel, appeared
in 1937, and was adapted for Broadway in 1939 as *The World We
Make*. In 1948, with Frank Partos, he received an Academy Award
nomination for his screenplay adaptation of Mary Jane Ward's
novel *The Snake Pit*. Brand's association with members of the
Hollywood Ten led to his questioning by the House Un-
American Activities Committee; he refused to cooperate, invoking
the Fifth Amendment. From the early 1950s to the early 1970s,
Brand was an editor at Crown Publishers. His other novels
include *The Heroes*; *Albert Sears*; *Some Love, Some Hunger*; and
Savage Sleep. He was also the author of *Local Lives*, a book of
poems about the Pennsylvania Dutch; a posthumously published
account of his participation in the 1977 Peace March from
Nagasaki to Hiroshima; and the text to *Fields of Peace*, a book
of photographs by George Tice.

PETER CAMERON is the author of three collections of short
stories and five novels, including *Andorra*, *The City of Your Final
Destination*, and *Someday This Pain Will Be Useful to You*.

THE OUTWARD ROOM

MILLEN BRAND

Afterword by
PETER CAMERON

NEW YORK REVIEW BOOKS

New York

THIS IS A NEW YORK REVIEW BOOK
PUBLISHED BY THE NEW YORK REVIEW OF BOOKS
435 Hudson Street, New York, NY 10014
www.nyrb.com

Library of Congress Cataloging-in-Publication Data
Brand, Millen, 1906–1980.
The outward room / by Millen Brand ; afterword by Peter Cameron.
    p. cm. — (New York Review Books classics)
ISBN 978-1-59017-359-6 (alk. paper)
1. Psychiatric hospitals—Fiction. 2. Psychiatric hospital patients—Fiction. 3.
Mentally ill—Fiction. 4. Mental illness—Fiction. I. Title.
PS3503.R2576O87 2010
813'.52—dc22

                        2010016519

ISBN 978-1-59017-359-6

Printed in the United States of America on acid-free paper.
10 9 8 7 6 5 4 3 2 1

CONTENTS

THE OUTWARD ROOM

To Pauline

For to him that is joined to all the living there is hope.

—ECCLESIASTES

Think then, my soule, that death is but a Groome,
Which brings a Taper to the outward roome,
Whence thou spiest first a little glimmering light,
And after brings it nearer to thy sight:
For such approaches doth heaven make in death.

—JOHN DONNE

PART ONE

I

SHE ALWAYS woke up early. Often a bell far away in the little group of buildings where the doctors in residence lived woke her, or a particularly loud note of a bird penetrated her sleep and left her listening. This morning she heard a nurse's step on one of the walks outside; she followed the receding sound. The air was gray, sunless just before dawn, it was only light enough to take the darkness from her room. In its half-light, clean of thought, she lay looking at the indistinct furniture—her dress over a chair, the door of the wardrobe a black crack—but hardly seeing it. More than not seeing. It was peace. Untouched, she kept looking steadily ahead of her. At a certain moment, the room changed. Like footlights flooding up a curtain, the sun filled it, the full light folded out and down and in the trees there was the loud sound of the birds. A wave of light and in spite of her will, she looked up and saw, shattering her, the bars.

She turned her head into her pillow. Remorselessly the bars were behind the white linen against her eyes. The pillowslip became a nurse's white skirt, and on it she saw a large ring of keys, a hand lifted the keys, and the nurse with known movements unlocked and went through a door. Unlock and lock, down corridors of endless doors. She put her closed eyes against her hands, holding out the sight, but the ring of keys became a ring on her finger. The ring burned, she opened her eyes again to the sun, and sight faded out.

She began to dress, keeping her back to the window and the rising sun. She let her nightgown slip to the floor and the chill of

9

the April morning entered her and she stretched for a moment with her breasts pulling against her arms. Her heavy hair slid black across her shoulders as she leaned down, angle of her knee, the thigh shadowed and the light flooding around her hips and narrow waist. Body that had lain in the warm baths, the running water holding her in hours of blanched calm. Now dry and free— her flesh was firm and cool. When she was dressed, in a smartly-cut dark blue dress—the administration believed in the therapy of clothes—she sat on the edge of the bed. It was too quiet to move. She looked at her legs; they were hard, nicely formed, with good ankles and calves. Why should she be interested in her appearance? A question Dr. Revlin would like. Were there degrees of death? Miss Barrett. It was a long time, she suddenly thought, since she had looked at her face. Had it changed her; each time she wondered whether it would alter her but it never did. Although half-afraid, she determined to look. Hidden in the wardrobe was a circular face mirror which Miss Cummings had given her. "It's too small for me," Miss Cummings had said. "It would fit you." She went and got it. Still half-afraid, she held the circle of reflection up and looked into it. She saw her face split by the dark line of heavy eyebrows. It was her face; the total form was hers. She looked more closely for the details. Her eyes, the same brown almost black; the sockets of her eyes were hollower than they would be in a few months, but that was not what she was looking for. She looked carefully at the skin; it was what it had been. Her nose and nostrils formed the same line she remembered; her mouth, most important, was unchanged—it was impregnable.

She put the mirror away and went to the window. In the trees were the loud birds, the spring. She made the bars disappear and looked at the sun, it blinded her and she thought of her brother. In a few days it would be his birthday. b. April 14, 1906—d. Other dawns broke in her throat and reaching out her hands she took the bars, holding them. Imprisoned. Without turning she saw the bed. I. H. On the pillowslip. They gave it a nice name,

Hospital. Death within, she was walled closer than in the walls of the skin. And yet, beyond the fence, outside, was the world— somewhere there was life.

Seven years. She dropped her hands. She could remember even the first slow becoming aware of it, after her brother's death. She too had died, but her death was not the peace the tombstone said, but a struggle lasting until exhaustion. From this quiet she slowly was remade, as if with pity, to a new kind of existing. In it, she reached backward to her brother. Horrified by the first sight, she tried not to think of him. She went still further back to find him, but always knowing a false movement in time would drop her full upon him, undefended, at the moment of his death.

Seven years, plunging again and again into blind struggle and agony and emerging. It was hard to decide which contained greater suffering, the months of black horror, of nothingness, or the retaking of life. As slowly over her weaving in the Occupational Therapy room she began to see clearly the gaze of nurses, of doctors, a new agony replaced the agony of the abyss. How careful they were with their concealing words—"sick," "recovered." She told herself, I'm insane. Periodic insanity, death in her blood. And they knew, they never stopped knowing. The other recovered patients knew too and the pity and knowledge was in them. Always the bars, the locked doors, the enclosed porches, the high picket fence, revolving stamping its lines behind tables, walks, trees. She was imprisoned in death.

In death, she had found herself a refuge, this room. The room in which she was now, was in a wing of a building given over to the hopelessly insane. The women on this floor, in the rooms off the corridor with its locked stairway doors, were harmless, their minds completely lost, rifted away in little distortions and vagaries they never saw. And as they were not aware of their own state, they were not aware of hers—a democracy of the dead. It had been difficult for her to get permission to stay here; Dr. Revlin had finally given it to her, for other reasons than that for which she had wanted it.

The floor now was peculiarly quiet, silence extended to its ultimate moment of breaking. As the sun rose higher and the dawn lifted into fuller light, she heard a faint step in the room across the hall from hers and heard the whirring circular scratch of a phonograph record followed by its shift into music. It was Miss Cummings greeting the day with a dance record. The record scraped steadily, unrolling the beat of jazz, until near the middle a worn groove switched the needle back and four notes were repeated over and over with jagged monotony. She heard Miss Cummings push the needle onward and the record continued again unbroken to the end. When the needle had slid off into hissing silence, Miss Cummings set it once more at the beginning. This repetition of records was the only pleasure she knew, to play them over and over for hours at a time. Sometimes, although she was heavy and awkward, she tried to dance to them, circling in the small space in her room. It made her happy, she was never tired of it. From being played so much, the records frequently wore out, but she had a sister who brought her new ones.

As if started by the dance record, other sounds began on the floor, steps, sounds of furniture touched or moved. Soon Miss Barrett's tottering steps came down the corridor. From fear, she stood rigid. Miss Barrett several times a day went from her room to the bathroom, and always dressed as if she were going outdoors in the cold. From the bundle of a heavy coat, a fur, a thick hat covering all but her eyes, the mute eyes looked out blank as if Miss Barrett inside had died. It was like something killed. Nonrecognition, seeing without sight. Before these eyes and the little tottering steps that expressed too the noncontrolling being, there could be no hope, outgoing, or warmth. Miss Barrett was the one person on the floor who made her afraid.

Miss Cummings was different, she could be a friend. Sympathy, many of the capacities of the living were still hers. She often came in to visit, and they talked together. "I see by my paper this morning that my friend the Pope," she said. But in between was straight ordinary talk, of weather, of nurses, of food. She had a story of her operation. She believed she had once had her liver taken out by a famous surgeon. The surgeon, after the operation, put her liver in his icebox. At supper his wife served some meat and he complimented her on it. "Where did you get it?" he asked. "Why from the icebox where you left it," his wife replied. This story gave her great satisfaction.

Miss Barrett's steps came back down the corridor and her room door opened and closed. The dance record went on and on, occasionally, as the machine unwound, swerving unharmoniously towards silence, and then under Miss Cummings' firm grinding of the handle, regaining its full beat. The sun seemed fixed at the horizon, and a calm—made by the repeated record—fell upon the world. She gazed through the window and as in rotogravure saw smoke seep up from factories, horses go to the fields, men walk along streets. She felt her legs planted on the floor and looked down at her immobility. If he had not died, it would be her world. Her world? She dropped suddenly to her knees and began to sob.

The record stopped and in its silence she heard Miss Cummings' door open. Miss Cummings came slowly to her. "What is it, dear," she said; she leaned over her and picked her up. "Perhaps it's the weather," she said and seeing in a moment that she was about to stop crying, tactfully left.

2

Sitting on the edge of the bed, she looked downward passively at the floor. The storm of longing and deprivation that had shaken her had left her; she was able to think more quietly. In the way she sat, looking down, she felt a repetition of her recent months in the depressive ward. It was better to retreat there for strength than to give way—to give way was to go back, to the terrible beginning of the cycle and its convulsive darkness. The surge of longing that had overcome her was a part of emerging from depression; she understood it, yet feared it as an echo of the manic state. That was what she feared, any return, even by implication, to the "manic." Darkness, the suction of her death—horror "O God don't, home, home, I want to go home"—was Stoney her voice the hours "Says he" loud "and I shot, shot, intercede, O Mary, home." Darkness, hard, a wall VISITORS ARE REQUESTED NOT TO GIVE MATCHES TO THE PATIENTS the red light, slow puncture of fear, began in the corridor and she knotted the bedclothes for protection; the arm approaching, but when the lights went on, Miss Regis said, "You know who this is, Miss Regis. Be quiet now." The train roar. Sometimes she saw her brother in all the violence of, but she must not remember; and sometimes there was a dull pounding, that was Miss Batras at the coffin, Miss Batras who was death. If in time she could rub the monogram I. H., Islington Hospital, from the pillow, but there was no time; she must escape. Now in the corridor, the hard hand took her, Now

die. "Why have you left your room? I'm Miss Regis, you know—"
"Where is death?" Again, "Let me hold this glass," Miss Regis
said. "It's paraldehyde; it will make you sleep."

3

STILL sitting on the bag, she remembered a day of her childhood, which, although only a few years of actual time separated her from it, now seemed almost forgotten. Her brother and she had set out together one day to go fishing; they fished occasionally in a small stream near the town where they lived. She was only nine years old and small and delicate for her age—the hair which she now kept cut to shoulder length then poured dark and lanky down her back. Her brother was older, was large and strong; as he walked beside her, she felt privileged just to be going with him, yet she knew that he was glad she was with him and that part of his pleasure was giving his attention to her. The day was hot; she remembered the haze of fields of timothy they passed and the trembling of trees when the sun was behind them. There was a threat of thunder; a few webs of cloud in the sky at some time of the day would solidify into storm.

"Try here," her brother said as they came through some brush out to the stream. They baited and dropped their hooks together; the hooks sank out of sight. As she stood looking down at the stream, as minute after minute went by and they got no bite, she began to lose interest; as she sometimes did, she began to day-dream. She thought of the future. Like any child, her thoughts were indistinct and vast; they excited her. All that she had read in books, all that she realized intuitively from the indications that came down to her from adults, all the surmise that bred with fiery heat in her blood rose within her. And suddenly she was afraid.

She called to her brother. He turned in surprise, expecting her to say something. What she had wanted to say was, "I'm afraid. You'll always be with me, won't you?" but it was impossible for her to say it. She continued to stare at the water.

4

At breakfast Miss Cummings sat next to her. She was particularly thoughtful, and asked her more often than usual if she wanted sugar. After the fruit, a wheat cereal she knew Miss Cummings disliked was served. Miss Cummings ate it slowly, clicking her spoon against the side of the heavy bowl, and at last said, "The food could really be better, but I suppose it's all one could expect for the money."

The dining hall was a bare room with a long table, high walls, and a double door at one end through which the kitchen could frequently be seen. Bare as it was, occasionally somebody got up and as if detecting an irregularity in the room, walked away from the table and came back. It troubled her when something like this happened; she always felt glad when a meal went through without incident. Occasionally it was worse. Miss Cummings once tried to exchange places with a mild-mannered woman named Miss Garabrandt. Miss Garabrandt resisted and Miss Cummings, with restraint, said to her, "You look like somebody I don't like." She remembered this because later, with no apparent connection, Miss Cummings had said, "My mother had dark hair, like Miss Garabrandt," and Dr. Revlin had made her tell this remark to him. She had had it in her mind and he had insisted that she tell him. She knew things like this were what he wanted her to see here, and were one of the reasons why he allowed her to stay here with the incurable cases, but she wanted to forget that there was any meaning to what they did or said, and to think of Miss Cummings and the others only as dead. It particularly irritated her to have Dr. Revlin find this significant proof of his theories in Miss Cummings, who was her friend. "You said such a thing could go by opposites," she said. "Maybe it means Miss Cummings was really fond of her mother." "Do you think so?" he said.

Always at breakfast she began to think of him. The peace, the other agonies even, gave way to him. She separated him from the other doctors, nurses, "recovered" patients, who knew. He was something different from them, a different face, voice. Voice, so much a voice. Trusted? Lately her feelings towards him had changed. What was it? Trying to find out what the change was, she went back—

Ever since he had known her, he had taken more than a routine interest. "Case," that was it at first. Then professional pride, generosity? She had to admit there was generosity. A long and difficult analysis. Yet the feeling she had towards him was not in this. Doubt. How did she feel? Lately at each talk with him—

She knew he was kind, open with her, but he kept her at times from fully understanding certain things about herself, that was it—she felt she had never found out completely all that he knew, that he was leading her up to something.

Miss Cummings nudged her shoulder. "Eat, my dear," she said. She realized she had been staring fixedly at the wall opposite, thinking. She finished her breakfast and tried not to think of Dr. Revlin again. "Drink your coffee," Miss Cummings said. "It will do you good." She drank her coffee and a few moments later a nurse took them upstairs. As they went up, Miss Cummings walked heavily at her side, helping her, holding her elbow. At the second-floor landing, the nurse lifted a key from a ring, opened the lock of the heavy door, and let them inside. In the corridor, daylight came only through the doors of rooms that stood open— Miss Barrett's door was always closed.

"You feel all right now?" Miss Cummings said.

"Yes, I do, thanks."

She left Miss Cummings and went alone into her room and from across the corridor she soon heard a new record beginning to play. She wondered if it were through thoughtfulness that Miss Cummings had changed the record, not to remind her of what had happened before breakfast. The record wound on and on, the little stylus grating with saxophone and horn. One phrase played into a fixing memory; the line of lifting chords, a quick beat, became joined in her mind with the wide stone of the stairs, the darkness of the corridor, and everything that made up this place, this moment. Memory. She thought how often, in Dr. Revlin's office, she had known some moment of the past to come into her mind as clear as this one now, and not just one but many moments so that they could be placed side by side. "What was his name?" "I can't remember." "Think, what was it?" "Cam—Cal— I can't." "It's there. Keep trying." "Lambert." Relentlessly in, farther and farther. Everything was there, and just as she found a forgotten name, other things came, closer, stronger, until they burst into consciousness.

Even more than in waking, in her dreams the things he wanted came.

Thinking. Thinking. She must stop thinking. The record played its mounting phrase, at the peak it started to die, falling away through key after declining key. Quickly Miss Cummings caught it, turned the crank and pushed it up to its original speed. Record, Dr. Revlin. All that was in her mind he touched with dream, association—listened. When she slowed, fell from full key, he knew it and—

She pressed her hands to her forehead. Stop! Stop! Far off, she heard a scream. Silence. Scream. O brother, she thought, if you had not died— Before her grew the world, cities, all the outside where there was life. Here nothing changed, there had hardly been any change in her body, nothing that took place in the living had taken place in her. Innocent and dead. She felt of a thin-banded ring she wore that her brother had given her and thought back seven years to the spring before his death. Birthday. All the earth now ripening to his birth, the buds opening his life again. "They lay hold on bow and spear; they are cruel, and have no mercy—" Quickly she got up from the bed and went towards the door, intending to go out. There was the sound of a nurse's steps in the corridor. No. She would be aware; she would see him dead. She stood and waited. The steps stopped; the nurse then was going to come into her room. She turned, facing away from the nurse as she came in. "A letter for you." She made no move to take it; the nurse left it and went out.

What could the letter be? The world beyond the fence had so long ago dropped from her, she believed it lost. Standing with her back to the window, she stared into the room— It could not be from her parents, not from them, they knew she would not want to hear from them. She went across the room and picked the letter up.

It was from her mother.

Darkness, death filling the room.

She read

"Dear Daughter, It has been a number of years since we wrote to you. As you know, Dr. Revlin asked us not to, during his treatment. We are writing now with his permission." Anger— "Dr. Revlin suggests that in a month or two we come to visit you."

She had been right. There had been something. Dr. Revlin— She folded and unfolded the letter. What did it mean? It had something to do with what she had feared. She went to the bars at the window and looked out. She drew back. In spite of fear, she must speak to him.

Miss Cummings stopped playing the record.

5

"HELLO," Dr. Revlin said as she entered his office, getting up and taking her hand. "It's a nice day, isn't it? Have you been out?"

"No—"

He noticed. "Something is troubling you," he said.

"Yes."

"What?"

She was suddenly afraid to speak.

"Yes, tell me. We've been through much together, haven't we? And I'm your friend, no?"

She said, "You are."

"You'll tell me then?"

"May I tell you afterward?"

He hesitated. "All right," he said.

She lay down on a couch, according to their routine, and he drew a shade, darkening the room. He sat down to one side, out of range of her sight. All she knew of him now was his voice.

"As you've something important to tell me later, we'll get right to business. Let's hope this won't interfere; for the time being put it out of your mind."

He waited.

"What did you dream last night," he said.

"Nothing."

"Resistance today. Or is it—? No, try to remember."

"I'm sure I didn't dream—"

"You've remembered before when you thought you hadn't dreamed. Try to think."

"I can't." Yet she was yielding, her mood changing. She said, "When I woke up, there was nothing in my mind. I even forgot I was in the hospital."

"That's interesting. Tell me a little more about it."

"That's all, I had just forgotten."

"No, how was it—did you feel you were home, before you came to the hospital?"

"I don't know, I didn't think of anything. But I was happy."

"Good! You were happy and didn't realize you were in the hospital. When you wake up and find you are in the hospital, you're unhappy, is that right?"

"In a way."

"Why 'in a way'?"

"I—all right, I'm unhappy."

"I wish you could tell me what you meant by 'in a way.' I want to know."

"I can't, I don't know."

"Let's try again. If you had woken up at home, before you came to the hospital, would you have been happy?"

"Yes, you know that!"

He paused. "Then you would like to be the way you were then."

"I know what you want to make me say. Can you bring back my brother?" she said.

He sighed.

"Let's start again differently. Suppose now, right now, you woke up somewhere and were not at the hospital—would you be happy then?"

"Yes, in a way—but not as happy as the other way."

"Why would it make you happier now, to be out of the hospital? Do you mean you want to be well?"

She said nothing.

"Would it be just that it meant you were well that would make you happy?"

"Stop!"

"You would be happier if you were outside, whether you were well or not?"

"Yes."

"But why?"

"Isn't there reason enough? Here everybody knows, they see my brother's death, my own death."

"You're not dead."

She said nothing.

"If you were not well, you would have to come back."

She still said nothing.

"Outside then you would forget your brother's death?"

"No, I'd—have it alone, for a while."

He waited a minute and said, "Is there any other reason why you would be happier outside?"

"No."

"You're sure? Be honest."

She hesitated. "Yes," she said.

"To have escaped me, could that be it?"

She felt her face flushing. "Yes."

"Tell me, had you thought of trying to escape?"

"Please, Doctor—"

"Tell me."

"I've always thought of it—not seriously, perhaps."

"All thought is serious. And what you think about this is very serious." He paused. "Let me tell you something, there have been people who were about to undergo an operation, one that would mean life or death to them. At the last moment, with all the arrangements made, they take a train, go away somewhere—in order not to go through with the operation. Possibly that's what you want to do?"

"I see what you mean."

"I think you know we're reaching a kind of—that we're coming towards something. Perhaps what you are going to tell me is the same as what I am going to tell you. But first I'm interested in your dream."

"How can I think?"

"You can. Don't think of when you woke up. Think back into the night."

She lay quietly, her thoughts out of control. But she was experienced and kept pressing back, backward to the night. All thought would stop, meeting darkness—then begin again.

"Yes. I did dream. I was acting in a play, in costume, and I was taking two parts, at the same time." The dream formed before her eyes, sudden, spreading out. She could feel as much as see, it was hard to put into words. What she said would not be the dream, and it would be the dream. "Go on," he said. "As one person I was very tall, a giant—as the other I was very small. No, that isn't it," she said. "Yes it is! Go on." "I felt really that I was the tall person and somebody else was the small person, but it was myself too. Is that possible?"

"Yes. It's all just as you remember. Go on."

"The small person was my servant and I felt very scornful towards her. No—" "Yes, you were scornful. But tell me, was there anything—why, in what way did you feel scornful?"

"I don't know."

"This is important. Did you express it in any way?"

Farther in. "Yes." How did he know? "I took my servant's mail and opened it. I think I even read it to her and she couldn't do anything about it."

"That's very interesting. Was there anything else? Think of the dream carefully."

"We, that is both of us, were wearing a strange kind of clothing."

"What kind?"

"It was like a costume, like historical plays."

"Good. Can you remember anything else?"

"No."

"All right, let's see what we can do with it—does it mean anything to you?"

"No."

"Let's go over it. You're a giant and the servant is very small, what can that mean?"

"I can't think—no, I can't think of anything."

"How about the dress?"

"I don't think of anything."

"Try."

"Yes." It came to her suddenly. *Gulliver's Travels*.

"That's very interesting." He paused. "Yes, that must be it."

"But I didn't think of *Gulliver's Travels* in the dream."

"No. You just thought of it now. But there is some connection."

"Why? Anybody might have thought of it." She felt angry.

"Perhaps. But why Gulliver? Why not David and Goliath, or Jack and the Giant Killer—you see it isn't so simple. No, you thought of it because it really is connected with your dream. That's how it works, the laws are rather strong."

She said nothing.

"Now let's see if perhaps there isn't some connection. A giant—" He paused. "Is the giant Gulliver in Lilliput, or is it a Brobdignagian?"

"I don't know."

"I'd say a Brobdignagian, do you know why?"

"No."

"Perhaps you do. Think."

"The Brobdignagians made Gulliver a kind of servant, a slave. They kept him in a cage."

"Yes, that's what I was thinking of. By the way, you know your Gulliver very well. Did you read it as a child?"

"Yes."

"When?"

"When I was five or six, I guess."

"Did your father or mother ever read it to you?"

"My father."

"Were there pictures in the book?"

"Yes—oh, I remember. There was one picture, the hat, yes I can see it—it's the same as in the dream."

"What?"

"The servant looked like Gulliver in this picture."

"Well, now we're getting somewhere." He stopped. "Then let's go back. Why did you think you were the same person?"

"I don't know."

"This may be rather important. Try association."

After a long wait, she said, "One flesh."

"Why 'one flesh'?"

"We were the same person."

"Any more associations?"

"My father used to say to my mother, 'You're my better half.'"

Immediately, as if excited, he asked, "How young were you when you first heard your father make that remark, about the 'better half'?"

"I don't know, I can't remember that."

"Tell me this. You've mentioned before that your father was weaker than your mother. Could you have felt it when you were five, six?"

"Maybe."

"How did he seem weaker, at that time?"

"My mother always ordered him around. I can remember her doing that. Oh, I remember—the mail. She used to open his letters and read them—"

"So that's the letters."

"It made him angry."

"Is there anything more about the dream?"

"Yes, there's something. But I don't know whether it's worth mentioning."

He said irritably, "You know everything is worth mentioning."

"I remember how as the giant I wasn't entirely sure I was superior to the servant."

"Yes, that's good. It all fits together. Gulliver in the story had a good mind, he knew more than the giant. And haven't you sometimes admitted to me your father was a remarkable man, that he had a quality of mind, not practical, but still superior somehow to your mother's?"

"Yes—"

"You realize it now better than you did as a child."

"Yes, I do."

"Well, you've explained the dream to me. And I haven't forced you to, have I, except to make you tell me?"

"No, I agree that that's the meaning of the dream."

He paused. "And it's close, like most of your dreams, to the whole problem of your illness. I said before that today we were going to talk things over as we never had before. You want to do this, don't you? We're going to, as they say, put the cards on the table."

"Yes."

"I want you to let me do most of the talking for a while now, and just answer what I ask you. Is this arrangement all right?"

"Yes."

"You know for a long time certain things have kept coming up, recurring. I had hoped they would give you an understanding of yourself, without my help—without my telling you too much. And I think you've come near it, some of it you know and much more of it you must guess. But it isn't enough, you don't really know it. And so I think the time has come to go farther—to sum the whole thing up quite fully and plainly. I believe it's the best. You may not see it now, but some time you will. And I have in mind too something else, to help you. Now, have you enough courage, will you go through with it?"

"Yes, I will," she said.

"All right. Then I'll tell you. It won't be easy for you. I don't know how it may affect you; maybe you'll be angry and won't believe me at all. But I think you ought to have it stated, put before you. Try not to argue, just listen to what I say."

She remained silent, looking upward, waiting.

"Here it is, then. At the center of your dream, clearly, you became your mother, you were putting yourself in her place in rela-tion to your father. The letters, the 'better half,' everything shows it. It's just another proof of something I've told you, that almost all children go through a period when they fall in love with the parent, the one of the opposite sex. It's an old story now, well-known. And being in love with one parent, children are jealous of the other parent—you were jealous of your mother. During the period of your childhood represented by this dream, you were in love with your father, but not as much as at first. Already your father seemed inferior to you. Later you substituted your brother for him, who was stronger and took after your mother—"

"No!"

"Remember, it isn't a matter of belief now, just listen." He went steadily on, "At a certain age, towards the end of childhood, the child, daughter in your case, becomes reconciled with the mother in order to be freed from the father. Then she can find her love outside of the family—she is identified with her mother; she can reach full adult love." He paused. "As I told you, your brother was substituted for your father, but it would have made no difference. Unfortunately your brother's death occurred just when you were beginning to free yourself from him and because of it, you have never been able to go on, past his death."

"No, I can't believe it. It's just words, it's just the way you want it. It isn't like that in me."

"You know, I'm not basing what I say on this one dream. All the material, all I've uncovered, hundreds, thousands of details support what I've told you. You say it's the way I want it—that isn't fair. I don't care about theories—I'm not trying to prove a case, I'm trying to help you."

She said nothing.

"At least you've kept your promise, you've listened to me. You don't have to believe me now; just remember what I've said. Re-member it carefully." She heard him move in his chair. "And now we come to what I mentioned before—something else I've thought of, to help you."

"Yes—"

"In a month or so, I want you to have your parents come to see you."

"No!"

"I know how you feel towards your parents—you think they killed your brother, but I hope by the time they come, I can make you overcome this feeling. At least enough so that you can see them—"

"No, please!"

"You say your father was tired the day of your brother's death and asked your brother to drive the car. And so, remotely speaking, he killed him. However, no reasonable person—"

"He did!"

"Remember—"

"He had no right to have a car. We were always poor, never had money, and yet he kept the car. An old one, a death trap. And my mother let him. It was my mother's fault as well as his—"

"You can make it look the way you want, but it isn't that really. That's what you'll have to see. By the time your parents come— I'll tell you— This is the final thing I've wanted to tell you. In the situation in which you were placed, something you could not know happened. It's a very delicate thing to explain to you, and you must forgive me if I'm too blunt. You know that unconsciously you must have felt some guilt about your love for your brother—"

"No!"

"It must have been a very strong love, it must have been that to do what it did to you."

She was silent.

"So it was a help to you, when you had to make a new adjustment to life, to blame your parents. Unconsciously, you said, 'If I'm guilty, they're guilty too. They killed him.'" He paused. "I've been as honest as I can. It's been hard to tell you all this. I haven't wanted to hurt you. I hope when you see your parents, things will suddenly become clear to you. In the meantime, with what you know, your mind can be more at rest. You know there is nothing else now, nothing unknown. And I count on you to be brave, to go on working with me, not to try to escape. Tomorrow, much of the pain of this talk will be gone. You'll find that your father's intelligence, which you have, will begin to help you. And this is very important—remember, even if this experiment I'm counting on fails, even then you can still have hope."

6

WEEK BY week the Earth broke greenly into spring. She watched foliage, like a fog, spread in the trees. It was not birth, Dr. Revlin said, it was knowledge. "Something is hidden and must be found, as in you yourself." It seemed that now they went beyond where they had ever gone before. "Then what did your father say?" "Were there?" "Why do you remember?" And she— "He let me play with his knife and—" "My father tried to stop me and he said, 'Run,' and—" Phonograph turning, coming closer and closer to the center. She was increasingly fearful; she was so afraid that only the final decision she had taken made her go on. "You won't be like those," he said, "who run away."

Particularly during this month, Dr. Revlin went over with her her relation with her parents. He told her that a great deal might depend on her visit with them. "Something may happen. I'm hoping—"

He made her herself write a note, in answer to her mother's letter. It was a difficult experience. She sat at his desk and he prompted her. "When shall—what date?" "Do you think two weeks?" he said, leaning over and thumbing the pages of his desk calendar. "Suppose we make it Sunday the twenty-first." "All right, the twenty-first." She tried the pen; the ink ran. "Dear Mother, How shall I say it?" "Just say it naturally, not formal." She went on writing. "Dr. Revlin—thinks that Sunday—the twenty-first of this month—would be a good time—for you and Father to visit me—Shall I say anything more?" "If you just said, 'I'll look forward to seeing you,' it might make them happy." "I'll look forward to seeing you," she wrote. Quickly laying down the pen, she got up. "You haven't signed it," Dr. Revlin said. "Oh yes." She sat down and signed the letter and he gave her an envelope and made her address it.

Now that a definite day had been set, all her thought concentrated on that. When she was alone in her room, she listened to the sounds outdoors, or to Miss Cummings' records, or to any sound that came to her and it was like a draft in her blood. What will I do?— She thought of the features of her parents, hard to remember. She could remember voice, physical gestures more easily. Sometimes she shivered with hate, other times not.

She made a definite effort not to give way to hate, she pushed the hate down—refused to think of it. She developed a trick that helped her. On her brother's birthday, a week after she had received her mother's letter, she had thought of her mother. Birth. Once a woman had been brought to the hospital who had been driven out of her mind by childbirth; at times she would think she was beginning labor pains and the shrieks she gave, even to her, were terrifying. Her mother had gone through that for her brother. Could she then—? But her thought stopped. When she wanted, now, to push down the hate, she remembered the woman who had thought she was in childbirth.

For several days just preceding her parents' visit, Dr. Revlin talked a long time with her. At the end of his long talk, he told her all that they had done and all that he hoped for for her. "I don't think there's anything more I can do to prepare you. It will help to have a little rest, even to forget me. Stay in your room, lie down. An important moment of your life is coming; believe that it will be for the best." He took her hand, and pressed it in encouragement. "Just one more thing. Forgive me for saying it—but don't hurt them. That must not be."

When the final night came, before the visit, she was continually restless. She was a long time going to sleep and when she finally got to sleep, she had a peculiar dream—it duplicated an experience of her childhood. One summer she had been visiting somewhere in the country with her parents, and had gone alone to play in a stable. With a child's daring, trying to see how far its courage will go, she had started to climb down from a hay chute into an empty stall. She meant to catch her feet in a metal feed trough and to get down that way, but as she swung from the edge of the chute, she couldn't reach it. She tried to climb back and found the hay silt had made the loft floor too slippery for her to get up. She began to scream. It seemed to her that she hung time-lessly, weakening and hanging over an abyss, when her father ran in and caught her.

In the morning, remembering the dream, she thought of Dr. Revlin, but thought, I won't have to tell him. The time for telling dreams, for inquiry, for doubt, is gone. Now, only a few hours ahead, was the certainty.

At eleven, a nurse came and took her to the visitors' room to wait for her parents. With the unrelaxing vigilance of the hospital, even here the door was locked. Its heaviness, the fact that it was locked, took away any illusion she might have had of freedom. She stood looking out of a window, and listened for the footsteps that would tell her her father and mother were coming. She breathed, pressing her breath carefully to keep it silent. Below her were the grounds, silent; a few trees that had dropped their rusted blossoms or strings of pollination, a bed of iris breaking sheathed bloom. Birth. As she stood waiting, she began to feel something at her heart. Not altering the silence, the shriek of the woman out of childbirth flowed into her. In my brother's death, she thought, you were made childless. Childless because I died too. She looked at the trees and at the furling blooms of the iris. A breeze moved them; she heard the sound of steps...

When she turned, a tall man, hollow-eyed, was looking at her as if frightened. Beside him was a smaller, firm-looking woman whose look was like her brother's. She said, "Mother—" Her father came across the room and took her in his arms. She let him. The room with its bare walls, paint. If it were not here, with locked door, the locks, separation— "Father!" He touched her hair, the separateness was still there.

They began to talk, they felt each other's voices. They talked of life, of how her father had work now, not making much, but better than what he used to have. "We think of you, we love you," he said. Her mother told her, hesitatingly, They had moved away from the town where they had lived when— A wish began to grow in her, a terrible wish, one that she could not hold back. In a momentary silence, she said, "Could I ask you something?" "Yes, of course," her mother said. "Where is my brother buried?" She saw the shiver of pain; her mother conquered it and told her, described the grave. You have wept there, she thought, It's the place of your death. When her mother had finished, they sat silent, brought together for a moment.

Her mother said, "You'll come home to us?"

Something that seemed near a junction separated. "No," she said, "I can't—" She looked at her mother, and saw her eyes pitiful with longing. "I can't, I can't." Longing? It was a lie. Beyond her power, everything began to break, everything changed. "You killed him!" All at once she realized that speech was pouring from her without control. They had killed him; she knew it. Her mother's eyes lied.

"Go away," she said at last.

7

Spring tightened against the Earth, and she tried to forget. She had a new nurse, Miss Child. Miss Child had only recently gotten her cap in a general hospital, and seemed different, less impersonal than the older nurses. She was dark and slight, with regular features and close-cut hair that waved in a short curve around her forehead and sometimes dropped in her eyes. Her voice was young and kind.

As they talked together, she learned that Miss Child had gone through the nurse's long hard course of study "to live my own life." "Of course," she said, "I liked the work too, but what I wanted most was to have something, a profession, that would make me independent." This nurse, to be independent, to live her own life, had come here, to this hospital, the place that to her was a place of death.

Being twenty-two, almost the same age as she was, Miss Child preferred her to any of her other patients. In the mornings, she would often come to take her for a walk through the grounds. When she wanted it very much, she would bring her a meal to her room and sometimes eat with her. She also helped her in her studies; Dr. Revlin wanted her to go through some high school textbooks: English, advanced algebra, French. Miss Child talked with her a little in French. Whenever she said, "*Et pourquoi?*" it reminded her of Dr. Revlin. She had once heard him speaking in French with his wife and he had used that phrase, in a humoring tone of voice. Her own French was not good, and she had no real interest in her studies.

She was thinking of Miss Child one morning, hoping that she would come, when she knocked on the door. "Come in," she said. It was something she liked in Miss Child that she always knocked; many of the nurses thought it unnecessary. "I was hoping you'd come," she said. "Why, do you want to go for a walk?" She frowned. "I didn't mean it that way," Miss Child said. "A day like this, why not want to go for a walk?"

She put on her hat and a worn leather jacket. They went together out into the hall, to the stairway door. She watched while the ring of keys was lifted and the door opened. At that moment Miss Child became a nurse. They went on down the stairs and Miss Child came back from the nurse's uniform to a girl again and was speaking in her resonant, alert voice. She said she had had a quarrel with one of the doctors. "Who?" "Dr. Thompson." He had been speaking the day before of why we enjoy a warm bath, he said pompously it was because it reminded us of the softness and protection of the womb and its amniotic fluid. "How do you know that—you can't know that," Miss Child said. The doctor disliked being contradicted by her. "All these theories of everything going back to the womb, it's nonsense," she said. They went out the side door of the building and along a cement walk. Sun, the far smell of summer. Dr. Thompson. Dr. Revlin disliked him. She thought of Dr. Revlin. After her parents' visit, he had asked her to come to his office. She had come in with a hard face. "So we failed," he said. He seemed irritated in spite of himself. Then sorry. "There is no hope now," she said. "There is always hope," he said. Their daily talks had begun again, but now without her feeling hope or fear. One day she said to him, casually, "I still want to escape." "You might as well," he said, smiling. "We've tried everything else." Then immediately he stopped smiling.

Restlessly, she wanted to walk faster and Miss Child quickened her pace. They were quiet, a companionship of silence in a world of ruin. The buildings were red brick, discolored and rimed by the rain and seasons, with the blot of the enclosed porches black against their sides. Far off on one side was a long low building that had no porches, the manic ward. Once when through curiosity she had gone near it, she had smelled a bland horrible odor that can never be cleansed from such a building and heard the sound coming from it. She felt repulsion different from that she had felt when she was within it. It was as if she had never been there. Yet all of the buildings had their knowledge in her. As she passed each one—the Occupational Therapy wing, the library, the recreation hall, the laundry, the buildings where she knew the depressives were—the harsh knowledge came out to her. She saw in a wide, three-angled building halls and staircases in which dumb blank-faced women sat and other women mutely carried pails and mops and floorcloths...

On walks like this one she had at last begun definitely to plan her escape. There was a picket fence that surrounded the hospital, and she had thought that there was no escape unless she could get over that. It was several miles long, much higher than her head, and had the crossbeam holding the pickets at the top planed down so that there was no hand or foothold on it. Planning her walks patiently, she had examined it section by section along almost the entire length until she discovered a flaw in it. On a small gate near the southwest corner, the usual crossbeam had not been planed down and at this point the fence could be climbed. It was on this gate that her whole plan of escape was based. It was a plan that had little chance of ever being carried out, but as she had decided on it, she would not give it up. Her plan was to try the locked staircase door night after night in the hope that at some time a nurse might by chance leave it unlocked. Once she got past the door, she was sure she could get to the gate and climb it. Two miles from the hospital was a railroad—

"The air today reminds me of a trip I took to Vermont last year," Miss Child said. "It was about this time of year and I went with a nurse I was in training with who had an old Ford." "Yes?" "We had both been working hard all winter, twelve hours a day, and we got a week off together. She had an uncle with a farm up there, and we went there. All the way the air was like this and we slept one night in the car."

"I've been here seven years."

Miss Child's face reddened and she said, "I should have remembered."

"No— What was it like driving?"

"It was wonderful." She hesitated. "I remember especially that when we got to Vermont, it was about sunset and coming up a slope of a valley, a mountain ahead—it's hard to describe it—it was surrounded with light."

She thought of the sunset and light coming around the mountain and it was as if the outside world whirled from the tints of newsprint into something real. She stared across the grounds and between two buildings she saw the picket fence, gray even palings, a row of triangular points.

8

A few days later, after lunch, she lay resting on her bed. The day was warm and she had opened two buttons of her shirt and closed her eyes as the cooler moving air of her room swept over her. As so often happened, she heard a faint scream that kept being repeated and suddenly ended. Downward, in the succeeding drop, into silence. Amniotic, what had she said, the silence of the womb.

Her brother said that he had seen her born, in a country house with no doctor and he had handed the basins of hot water to her father.

Her birth, her death. So now changeless— She seemed still not to be a woman, in spite of her firm breasts and the roundness of her thighs. The years here had had little meaning, she had not changed. In death there is no change. And yet—

There was a knock on her door. "Come in," she said. Miss Cummings came in, her large figure emphasized by the door. She had on a lavender house dress and her hair was in a knot at the back of her head; she had a newspaper under her arm. "Sit down, Miss Cummings," she said, and drew a chair for her near the window. She had noticed during many visits that Miss Cummings liked to look out of the window. She took the chair and for a significant minute they were silent. Then, drawing the paper from under her arm, glancing at her as if she were about to impart some important confidence, and carefully opening the paper, Miss Cummings read, "FIRE MENACES ISLINGTON HOSPITAL A tool shed in Islington Hospital caught fire yesterday afternoon and spreading rapidly in waste and other inflammable materials threatened to set fire to one of the larger buildings. Fire equipment from Clifton and Houton answered the alarm and fortunately put out the blaze before serious damage was done. Fire Chief George Mercer of Clifton was complimented on his effective handling of the emergency." She paused dramatically and said, "I think that proves it, all right."

Immediately she guessed what Miss Cummings had in mind. For a long time she had been convinced that one of the employees of the hospital who ran the mowing machine on the lawns had "designs" on her; she was interested in him and rather pitied him. "He did it, of course," she said. "I suppose I should really report it to the Superintendent." She thought that he had done it out of desperation. "With such people this place is not really safe," she said. That morning, she added, she had seen him looking up at her window, with obvious meaning.

Before refolding the paper, she importantly read another story: "TWENTY BANKS REOPEN." When she had finished reading the short item, she said, "President Roosevelt is such a help. He had my sister's bank personally reopened."

She spoke about her sister and a son that she had. He was "a little difficult." If she were not perfectly comfortable here in the hospital, she would like to live with her sister, and help her with her son. They talked unhurriedly, with long spaces of quiet. Miss Cummings looked out of the window, yet always as if politely aware that she was with somebody, paying a visit. "Are you quite happy?" she said. "Yes." "It's much the same thing, to be here or with my sister I suppose."

She thought of the fire that had occurred the day before. The tool shed was near the ambulance garage, at some distance from the building she was in. The outside world had come to this world apart, because of the fire.

Under Miss Cummings' gentle voice, she lay back again on the bed. A nurse passed with a quick step in the corridor. Keys, the sound of doors. Revolving days, identical slow and empty with everything known. She looked up at the ceiling, a white plane meeting the walls running to the bars of the window. Home. No home—habitation, place. Nonexistence. Walking to the dining room, walking back. Thick cups and saucers, unchanging food. The nurses, courteous, and yet— The appropriation for the hospital was smaller than it had been and there were fewer nurses. They were worked harder and except for Miss Child, kept to themselves. Their own world, the unfaltering look of their eyes, the whispers overheard . . . "That Graham woman tried to drown herself today." "Did you hear about Elsie getting kicked?" Low voices of their other world against the voices issuing from the world of darkness, out of memory. "One two three four one two three four I want to see Dr. Stearns I want to see Dr. Stearns" monotony spurting from the bodies jerking over beds, the hands bound or emerging from the quiet of the sheets. And even this was as nothing against the horror in herself, in which darkness plunged and swayed and suffering lengthened slowly to rest. Apathy. She sat up and stared at the floor. Miss Cummings saw that something was the matter and, with her usual understanding, got up and went across to her own room. After an interval of perfect quiet, she heard the grinding of the phonograph handle and soon the needle swerved into jazz. As the record monotonously played, she thought no longer of its circling to a center, but only as going on and on, unchanging, in a continual unchanging repetition.

9

It was after supper, the still-early dark falling. Miss Cummings had just let her phonograph run down and she imagined she must be sitting looking out the window. Beyond her window and her own, a peculiar yellow light lay that sometimes came just after the setting of the sun; it darkened. Miss Child was coming, she was waiting for her. She listened through the undertones of the building for the click of her key and when it came, switched on the small light over her bed. Miss Child knocked on the door and opened it.

"You have no uniform?" she said.

"No."

"There's nothing wrong?"

"No." Miss Child frowned. "We're friends, aren't we?"

The dress she was wearing was dark, close-fitting, with two large wooden buttons and a straight-bar pin at the V of the breast. She liked it. They sat down together on the bed, and with the disappearance of the usual white uniform, the white stockings and shoes, a new feeling came between them—it was as if her death were denied. A different state existed, Miss Child could not understand it, at least not fully or knowingly. Although she had come to help her with her studies, they forgot the books lying on the bed and almost at once began to talk. She liked hearing Miss Child's voice; the pitch of it, the assurance, was not like the older nurses' voices. Miss Child asked if she had heard about the fire. "Yes, Miss Cummings told me," she said.

"It didn't amount to much. You should have seen how important the firemen felt, though. They chopped everything in sight." She laughed. They went on talking, of the fire, of an addition that was being talked about to the administration building, of a nurse— Miss Fisher. "Miss Fisher told me your parents visited you not long before I came."

"Yes."

"Do you mind my speaking about it?"

"I'd rather—I don't like to talk about it."

"I see."

"Do you love your parents?" she asked Miss Child.

"Yes," Miss Child said. She lay bent on the bed. "Although I wanted to get free of them, and it was hard for them to understand."

"How do you mean, 'free'?"

"Oh nothing. It was—"

"It was—" She stopped as though a hand had been placed over her mouth. A voice not her own— "At a certain age, the child . . ."

She reached up and put out the light.

At last she said, "You told me you lived in New York. Did you live in New York always?"

"Yes."

"In the city itself?"

"Yes. When I was younger, we lived on East Eighteenth Street, near Gramercy Park."

"What was that like?"

Miss Child described the street and the park. "The park had a high fence around it and the gates were always locked, except for people with the key—we used to play in Stuyvesant Park."

Almost interrupting, she said, "Tell me about New York City. It must have been wonderful; a child in the city, in New York City."

"I don't know— When you're a child, it's all right, you accept everything. You have almost nothing to put between yourself and what's around you—"

"I know."

"Later you think, 'How ugly the world is!' Afterward that changes too—and then you don't see anything."

"Why?"

"I don't know. No time, you haven't time to stop living and see."

She turned her head down. "I've stopped living," she said.

"I forgot. Dear, I forgot," Miss Child said. She touched her shoulder. "Please forgive me."

"This is a place of death. You can't understand. Sometimes—" She hesitated.

"What?"

"Sometimes I would do anything to get away."

"Escape?"

"Yes, escape."

"There is no way, is there?"

"No."

10

AFTER Miss Child had gone, she lay motionless, looking upward. It was early evening yet, but as dark as it would be all night. Through the partly opened window a ringing of crickets, sawing in the warm summer grass, went on monotonously. There is no way. An automobile somewhere in the grounds threw a momentary light in the room and she turned on her side. Lost. Across the black air, a scream began strangled down into silence. No way. She sprang up rigid. It was all around her again, she was alone. The years poured up in her with their whole terror; it was this, the hospital, on all sides its rooms, corridors, buildings thrust down against her. She shivered. Should she try the door tonight? She was almost afraid to move. At last she went slowly out into the corridor and down to the stairway door. At the door she stopped; it was the last terror. Knob. Would it—Slowly she reached out her hand, turned. Tonight? She pulled; slowly the door opened and beyond it she saw a black hollow—

Quickly she pushed the door shut again. She heard Miss Barrett's room door open, and in the dark corridor Miss Barrett, muffled in her wraps, came forward on tottering steps towards the bathroom. She lay back on the closed door. The steps veered past her and Miss Barrett's eyes stared ahead with their nonrecognition. Holding the coat she had on close across her throat, she disappeared into the bathroom.

She must be quick. She ran back to her room and stripped the pillowcase off her pillow. Hurriedly without switching on her light she opened the wardrobe and took out several dresses. She had three which would look like the present season's styles. From a drawer under the wardrobe, she took what remaining clothing she would need, folding each article quickly and putting it in the pillowcase. She had a comb her brother had once given her, of thin ivory; she put it in the center of the bundle. When she had quickly packed all she would need that she could carry inconspicuously, she took a leather jacket from the wardrobe and carefully wrapped the pillowcase in it. She also took a coat out and put it under the covers of her bed to make it look as if she were sleeping there. At the final moment, she felt of the ring on her finger.

Now, holding her bundle, she went to the door and listened a moment. Everything was quiet. She glanced back at her room, at the indistinct furniture, the apparently sleeping form in the bed. Escape. It was as if she had escaped already, as if everything were done. The large room with its pallid blocks of light and shadow was no longer real; it was like a room forgotten. She went out.

Miss Barrett was still in the bathroom. When she reached the staircase door, she hesitated. Miss Cummings. How would Miss Cummings feel if she went without saying good-by to her? Her hand detached itself; she forced herself to go to Miss Cummings' door and knock gently. She heard a rustle of covers and opened the door. Miss Cummings was sitting up in bed, looking at her; her look was matter-of-fact, pleased. She could see her plainly in the room filled with moonlight; a wide square of it covered half her bed. She went to her and said, "I wanted to say good-by." "I know. You're going now?" Miss Cummings said. "Yes." "I hope you have a nice trip." She put her arms around Miss Cummings, with all the affection she felt for her overcoming her. "Good-by," she said. "Good-by," Miss Cummings said. "I'll miss you."

At the staircase door again, she listened carefully. No sound. She pulled the heavy door open and saw a faint light. Holding her breath, she closed the door behind her and went forward to the edge of the stairs. Everything looked different. Unused to the steps by night, she found the electric light on them different from the grayer light of day. She put her hand on the metal bannister and started down.

She knew that at the bottom of the stairs was a cross corridor, one way leading to the downstairs main hallway in which was the clerk's desk, and the other leading to a door giving outside on the grounds. She decided it would be best if she tried to walk quickly and naturally, so that it might seem as if a nurse were coming down the stairs; to do it took all her will. When she reached the bottom, she hesitated for a moment and as she stood waiting, she heard steps coming down the main hallway. Whoever it was, she had only a moment now to reach the outside door. She ran to it, opened it, and went outside. The cool night air closed around her and she crouched back against the door. All the buildings of the hospital stood bright in the moonlight. It was different from seeing them from a window. Now they were bare and the spaces between them appeared greater; now there was no concealment. As she stood waiting, she heard steps inside the building coming towards the door. She thought, I can't run. They'll see me. She sprang to one side and lay flat on the ground in some tall flowers. The door opened and two nurses came out, in dark caps, with purple capes waving back from their shoulders. She looked at them over the flowers—the professional attitude, the sharp features as they spoke casually to each other. Without pausing, they walked rapidly away and soon she lost sight of them in the dark. She crept up from the flowers and holding her jacket-covered bundle under her arm, walked away with what confidence she could along the cement path after them.

This path led towards the south fence and she decided the best thing would be to get to the fence. There were few buildings near the fence and many trees grew along it. Once she reached the fence, she could walk in comparative safety to the gate at the western end. Ahead, though, were three buildings she had to pass. The first was the administrative building, and it was this that she was most afraid of. The walk went close to it, only a few feet from the ground floor windows. Fortunately the shadow of the building fell in front of it and a light was burning in only one window. She walked quickly along until she came into the shadow, like a projection of the building downward, concealing her. As she passed the lighted window, she glanced upward and saw several nurses talking together, in what seemed to be a rest room. Their voices had the cadence of all voices until they faded, cut off into silence. She hurried on. The farther front of the building was unlighted, with the blindness of night in its windows. As she emerged into moonlight again, she felt once more the remote distances of the grounds.

The next two buildings were dark with only one or two vague lights burning, through curtains that waved against unknown interiors. The enclosed porches, which she had never seen close in moonlight, threw webbed black shadows on the walls occasionally blurred with ivy. Fear slowly ebbed out of her and the ringing sound of the crickets welled up with the promise of vacancy and peace. There was still the fence. At the last building the cement path ended and she went across the grass, leaving as she went under trees the dimensionless spaces of the moonlight behind her. She was surprised at the silence. Already it seemed impossible that in the buildings behind her was the horror she knew.

The fence raised its pallid gray palings in the dark. She went close to it, looking through its narrow cracks at the cinder path and road beyond, illuminated at intervals by the white radiance of arc lights. The fence, the last barrier. She lifted her hand and felt the planed-down beam. It would be impossible to climb it here. Too high, its strong thick boards were as impregnable as a wall. She started walking along it, and watched the trees, thinking there might be one with a limb going out over the fence, that she might get over this way. There was none. She could hardly see the buildings now, in a few places a roof or chimney would loom up. She thought only of the fence. From the arc lights its palings threw long shadows on the ground that slanted towards her or away as she walked. On and on. This side was, she knew, over a mile long. As she was walking, quickly and softly, she heard steps.

Two women were coming along the path outside the fence, apparently nurses in the hospital. They must not see her. Quickly she stepped back behind a tree and they passed, not noticing her, not looking towards her. She could hear them talking, "so I said to Dr. Jones." She waited until their steps and voices had receded out of hearing before she continued on down the fence.

She passed one gate which had the crossbeam planed down, and tried it to see if it were locked. It was firmly locked. She walked on, her steps muffled by the soft ground. Endlessly the palings of the fence revolved beside her, the undeviating mark between her and freedom. Bars. They showed behind their even gray-painted surfaces shivering doors pounding fear. They whirled, receded, and advanced with the click of keys. Steps "you must sleep" the air foamed black in her and she felt faint. The buildings are behind me, outside of me. She stopped, holding herself quiet before she went on. Watching only the crossbeam of the fence, the line going on, everything else in blackness. She repeated, To be free. To escape. To be free. With her last strength, she came to the gate and touched its flat crossbeam.

It was as if a focus shifted. All the surroundings came clear and she stepped back into shadow beside the gate looking off towards two buildings fifty yards away. She must act quickly. At any moment a guard might come, or some change might endanger this last chance of escape. She knotted the sleeves of her jacket around her bundle in the pillowcase and threw it over the fence. There was nobody in sight. Reaching up, she grasped the crossbeam of the gate and leaping upward, got her knee upon it. She stood erect, her feet on the crossbeam and her hands holding two of the pointed palings. At this final moment, she gave one look back at the silent unnoticing buildings and the cricket-pulsing dark of the grounds. Leaning on the paling points, from which she protected herself with her hands, she twisted over and dropped down.

I I

HER FEET stung from the fall. She picked up her bundle in the jacket and walked quickly away along the road. Nobody was in sight, there was no sound. The dark paused from arc light to arc light, scattered under the leaves of the trees. Thin moths whirled and staggered above her head. She was unseen, free. But she must get away. At the end of the fence, the road turned off into a woods. It became dark, with only a faint moon to show the direction. Ahead, she knew, was a railroad station where many times in the distance she had heard trains stop. The last train through had been just before Miss Child left and she knew it would be after midnight before another train came. Lying sleepless in her bed, she had often listened at night to the trains and knew the night schedule. It was Wednesday and on weekday nights there were only two trains on this spur line, going between a nearby main line and a factory town twenty miles away. In her plans for escape she had always thought of "riding a train." How one "rode a train" she did not know, but she knew she would be able to do it. As she walked along, feeling the unevennesses of the road beneath her feet, sometimes half stumbling in the dark—she felt as if the dark altered the usual daytime relations of the body to the earth, and she went faster—she decided it would be too long to wait until midnight for the train, with the chance of her escape being discovered. She would walk along the track towards the junction in the outskirts of the nearby city, and try to get a New York train from there.

Ahead she saw a light and came to the place where the road crossed the track beside the station. The station was deserted, the ticket agent's window locked. One bulb burned in the waiting room. As she passed the station on her way down the track, she heard the click of a telegraph key sounding untended in the night. It died behind her and she stepped over one moon-still rail and began to pace the tracks, her legs going quicker on the short tie spaces. I am going. At every step, farther away, towards safety. Walking steadily, she followed the track around curves, past tiers of trees, in and out of a moonlight that was part of the air and moved along her legs. The moon was metallic, close. She could put out her hand and touch it; it burned against her head. Alone. In the dark alone. Tie by tie, step and step. Her steps were almost running. Under her between the ties were cut stones, slate-gray banked off at the sides. It was hard to keep her steps short. If she skipped ties, the stride was too long. After she had been walking a half hour, she came to a road crossing the tracks. She approached it carefully, but there was no watchman, only a warning bell on a post. She went on, steady, her breath pacing the ties. Dark, into the moon. She passed a water tank and crossed two more roads. She must be a long distance from the hospital now. A large building rose up close to the tracks. Beyond, the tracks flared out in many wide curves to a row of huge piles of coal. Cranes sprang against the night sky. Keeping to the main track, she walked ahead. Fences throwing black shadow hemmed in the tracks now. Sheds. Buildings. Soon she began to see lights and the first street crossed the track. Vacant lots. She was afraid now of being seen. At the next street, she walked away from the tracks and turned a corner walking down a long street that followed the railroad. Houses, here and there a light. Two men passed her, talking. She knew that if she kept going steadily ahead, in the same direction, she would reach the crosstracks of the main line going to New York. She came to the end of one street and had to go sideways to another. When she almost thought she had lost her way, she saw ahead the lifted black and white guardarms of a railroad crossing. Those great arms, reaching up, were like real arms, drawing from the sky and its darkness—concealment.

She approached the New York tracks cautiously and as she crossed them, looked down in the direction the station must be. About three blocks away she saw it, the radiance going out from the platform across the tracks. She went on and turned down a side street so that she would approach the station from behind.

I must get on a train now. She approached the station like an animal, sensing it, watching it with desperate intentness. It was lighted inside but the back, with its folded-up baggage ledges, its vacancy facing the street, was dark. She walked along a side of the station to the front. At the end of the front platform were several V-shaped trucks pushed together at different angles making a nest of dark. She stepped in among them and put down her bundle, crouching beside it in the dark. She could hear, some distance beyond her, two men walking up and down, talking.

She had been sitting, alert and listening, a quarter of an hour when she heard the first far-off sound of the train. From inside the station, men and women began to come out on the platform. The train whistle sounded, rising in a repetitive threat. Soon, she could hear the pounding beat of the engine. She picked up her bundle. A long hiss, candescence stiffly screaming to silence. "New York train!" Beyond her she could see the train end. Under the rear railing, suspended in a wide loop from flat black steel, was a length of chain. Men were loading baggage into the train. People were getting on board. At last, in a moment cold with premonition, two hisses sounded. The train started.

She had to do it. The force of her will, of hope, thrust her out running across the tracks. Holding the neck-high steelwork of the back platform of the train, almost at a leap she seated herself on the chain. Her feet stretched out ahead, and as the train increased speed, the chain swayed and held. She kept hold of her bundle by balancing herself with one arm—the city with its walls, fences, yards, fell and at last ended in the sameness of speed.

12

HER HEAD was below the level of the rear platform of the train. Light poured out from it, but she was in shadow. Looking downward, she could see the ties rushing under her like a liquid floor. Her feet were only a few inches above them, and there was only a little space between the ground and the understructure of the train. She thought, If my feet sank down and were caught in the ties. My legs would be crushed. Immediately she held her legs higher. The speed of the train became a threat, sweat ran under her arms. She saw the liquid ties rushing towards her. She swayed on the chain. The steel wheels on either side of her rolled smoothly on their great hubs.

If she could climb up, find some place to hide in the train. She thought of getting to the roof and clinging there. Even as she thought of it, with some slight belief that it might be possible, a conductor came out on the back platform. She pressed against the train in the shadow, seeing him but not being seen. He stared out over her head and after a moment sat down on the steps. She saw him light a cigarette and flick the match away, into the funnel of train wind. She glanced sideways and the earth sprang rushing against her eyes. She looked back again at the conductor, who was smoking with slow movements. He had a clean-shaven face and she imagined his lips smiled. He had children, she thought. The links of the chain bit into her flesh. After two cigarettes, he got up and went back into the train.

Now the links began to bite unbearably, no matter how she tried to shift. The pain ran down her legs, numbing them, and only cords drawn from her brain held them up. The ties, pouring under her between the great rushing wheels. She concentrated on her lifted legs. Houses flashed past, remote in the night and she knew there were roads, autos halting with headlights, but only her legs outstretched existed. Keep them up. Only till the next station. Miles revolving down the wheels, delivering her from the hospital behind. Each minute forward was safety; in getting on the chain, she had accepted pain—now beyond it was freedom.

The train rolled loudly out over a trestle; the ties opened, and she could look down between them. The night under her, trees and roofs of houses clear in the moon. Sound around her changed, lightened in mid-air; it was better in air. She leaned back. Gradually the earth lifted; the ground returned.

Her arms and back ached. Fixed on the swaying chain and looking down on the ties pouring under her, she began to lose thought, her suffering breaking even the limits of hope. There would be no end to this trip. The light over her, coming out from the platform, was as nonexistent as time and the passengers inside had never gotten on and would never get off. There was no use in holding up her legs. The ties poured towards her and she saw her heels go lower, pulled against furious force. She looked straight ahead of her, at the black steel indented with shadow. It would be now. Instantaneously one foot was wrenched under, her shoe toe burned along the ties. Not crushed, her leg not crushed; some unknown elasticity of her body had saved her. Strengthened from shock, she disengaged her foot and held it up again in front of her. The pounding onrush of the train carried her forward.

13

WHEN THE train stopped, with a jarring inter-colliding of coaches, she dropped off and almost collapsed on the tracks. Get away. Through a humming faintness, she saw that she was in another city station—at the end of the train in darkness. She must get away before the train pulled out and the light of the station reached across the tracks to her. She lifted her bundle under her arm and walked stiffly, stumbling over the intersecting tracks, to the first street crossing.

When she reached the street, she saw the city beyond the shadows of fences and buildings, slanting gradually away in the distance. She walked forward. White cement walls, store fronts closed with faint lights in their windows. She passed a poolroom and under a window-shade saw men standing holding cues in a haze of smoke. The streets trapped her; she must get to the country, to a hiding place where she could sleep.

To sleep. By now it was the only need she knew. She walked ahead, keeping to one direction, her steps sounding on sidewalks, curbs, pavements. At last the houses became fewer, ended. She saw ahead a patch of woods and struggled into it, out of everyone's sight. The moon burned, she tripped and fell. She closed her eyes almost before she put her head against her bundle.

Miss Cummings called to her from the window. She ran. They were hunting her. She climbed along the netted porches, hoping to leave no trace. She tried a door and strangely it was unlocked. She crossed a room to a door at the far side, opened it, went into a second room. No locks; the door behind her opened. At what she saw, she awoke thinking she had screamed.

Somewhere in the distance a dog was barking. It was daylight. Around her was a woods, no house, no road in sight. She sat up. Feeling pain in her right toe, she looked at it. A dusty smudge across the tip of the shoe. The ties. She pulled a handful of leaves and tried to clean the discoloration off, but it was roughened into the leather. Her legs felt sore, and her back too, as she got up. With the sun shining warm and black through her hair, she looked around. Except for the distant barking of the dog, she was islanded alone.

She felt thirsty. She picked up her bundle and began to walk. At first she thought of going towards the barking dog where there would be somebody to ask for a drink, but then she was afraid of being seen. She was not far enough yet from the hospital. She had no idea what means might be used to recapture her, but she was in terror. Police broadcast, radio broadcast? All today, she decided, she would keep hidden in the woods, and only at night try to get farther towards New York. New York, where Miss Child had lived. A city. A city in whose size she would be unnoticed.

To satisfy her thirst she would have to find a brook or spring. She made a wide circle around the barking of the dog, pushing through trees and underbrush. The barking ended behind her and at last, following a long slope downward, she found a brook that cut around some roots of trees in a bank of red shale. She kneeled down at the water's edge and drank.

In the water glistening past her black hair, she saw time moving slowly. A passage towards death? Life. I am with you now, brother. I have you alone. And yet she thought, Perhaps I have left him. And she thought of what Dr. Revlin had once said, that she had left him before: "You never shared his death completely, only death in life." The water moved almost motionless and broke against stones. On its surface her shadow fell, long and dark. Like an outline around it was the sun, a burning duplication. My brother. Brother, forgive me— Quickly she got to her feet and walked over the red shale into the wood.

As the day went by, she became hungry. She was thirsty again too, but stayed away from the brook. She lay outstretched on the ground and thought. What was it? Life? Or death? She could not know, and in fatigue and hunger turned to something less difficult. A name. She must have a name, now, for the world she was entering. Dr. Revlin's wife's name was Harriet. Harriet Revlin. No. For a last name she would take her mother's maiden name, Demuth. Harriet Demuth.

And in her mind a plan for the night began to form.

14

As the afternoon sun sank lower and its light was less hot and clear, she began to feel nervous. Hunger. She walked back and forth listening. No sound, only the cawing of some crows. The sun glittered through the trees, horizontal, fading. In spite of her fear of leaving the woods, she knew she must leave before nightfall. She started walking in one direction, keeping to it as nearly as she could by the sun. Brush, rocks, tree trunks. Detours, struggling back to the line of the sun. At last, through the woods ahead of her, she saw an opening and came out on a rutted dirt country road. In the indistinct sun now rapidly setting, she hurried forward and came to a paved highway where there was a signpost. Going close up to it, she read, among other names, NEW YORK.

It was her plan to try hitching rides in automobiles. She had once or twice begged rides that way as a child, and as she remembered, it had not been very hard. The best place to get a ride was at the top of a hill, where cars would be going slower. As she stood thinking, an automobile whirled rapidly past her. It would be almost impossible, she thought, to stop it going at that speed.

She walked down the road; the road continued level, and soon entered a small town. As there was little chance of getting a ride in a town, she went on. A sidewalk began and she passed a grocery store, with food shining in the window. Although the store was clean, it seemed a poor section of the town; a few people sat on slatternly porches and the side streets were vistas of poverty. At the end of the town where the road came out in the open, a hill rose in front of her. When she came to the top of it she saw that the road was under repair for a short stretch, and thought, This will help even more, as cars will have to slow up for the rough road. She sat on a white fence under a tree and waited. Some trees across the road concealed the night sky.

In the silence, the town below dropped away and she thought of the night before. Already another night had come, a day had passed. She wondered what had happened in the hospital, Miss Child questioned, other nurses talking. And how would Dr. Revlin feel about it? She remembered what he had said, "You might as well—" Did he really mean it? No, it was something to say, but the decision he could not take. And yet— Across her thought, the sound of a motor broke; a car was coming.

She watched it approach; in the dark she could not see it very well, but she signaled it; it slowed and stopped.

"Hurry up!" a voice said.

She ran quickly and a door swung open. "Get in." A man was driving the car, well dressed as far as she could see, with a low-turned hat and dark summer suit. He immediately started the car again, and when he was past the torn-up stretch of road, increased speed.

"Where you going, sister?" he said.

"To New York."

"Yeah!"

He looked surprised.

"Well, you can go along with me, if y' want to. I'm driving all night."

"All right."

He looked down at her bundle. Part of the pillowslip showed.

"Got friends in New York?"

"I live there."

"That so!" He accelerated the car, which hummed with an unrelaxing sound. "Not to be personal, how do you come to be—on the road? I mean you don't look like—"

"I was staying with some relatives—and they did something—they didn't treat me right, so I left."

"Just started home on your own, hey?"

"Yes."

"Well, that took guts."

The car climbed unslackening up a hill.

"Just leave?"

"Yes—"

"Where from, Coharries?"

"Yes." She began to worry, at his continued questioning.

"Who were you staying with there?"

"People by the name of Brown."

"Arthur H. Brown?" he said eagerly.

"No, another Brown," she said.

"Whereabouts do they live?"

"King Street," she said, fortunately remembering the name of a street she had passed.

"Oh, that neighborhood," he said.

He drove along silently for a few minutes and she was relieved, seeing that he apparently accepted her story. She looked ahead at the steady road-flooding headlights. The car, a large one, had no lights inside.

"Say, sister," the man said, "if anybody stops us, asks any questions, you're my niece, see? and leave the talking to me. Got it?"

"All right."

"Anything I say is right, see?"

The car moved around a curve unhesitating, its tires holding in a long whine. Her sight was lost in the onrush of the road, constant and undeviating as the man guided the car with little inch twists of the wheel or a slow pull for a curve. Faint with hunger, she let her head sink back, and with eyes only slits, watched the car bore onward.

She woke up feeling the car had stopped. "How about a cup of coffee?"

"Where are we?" she said. It was still dark and they had stopped on a city street.

"Oh, we're only about halfway there," the man said. He helped her from the car and she went sleepily with him into a cafeteria.

"Two coffees," he said. He glanced at her. "Do you want anything else?"

Anything else— She saw a pile of doughnuts. "Doughnuts."

"A couple of doughnuts for the lady."

Food. She ate hungrily and took a few sips at the coffee. It was hot. To her surprise when she looked up, the man had finished. She was embarrassed—she knew he was in a hurry. She took her cup in both hands and gulped the coffee which burned and strangled her. "Thank you," she said to the man, getting up.

At that moment, two men entered the cafeteria and walked slowly up to them.

"Your name McBain?" one of them said to her companion. He looked steadily back. "No," he said. "My name is Hessler, Charles Hessler. Why?"

"We just wanted to know. Got your driver's license?"

"Why," he said, with just a slight shade of indignation, "are you gentlemen—?"

"Yeah, we are," the other one said, opening his coat.

"All right, here it is."

"Okay. Who are you?" the first one said, suddenly turning on her.

"I'm Mr. Hessler's niece," she said.

"Where are you going?"

"He's taking me home, to New York."

"At two o'clock in the morning?"

Quick— "I just heard that my mother is sick—"

"Gentlemen, don't you think this has gone far enough?" her companion interrupted icily.

"I guess it's a mistake, Carl. Sorry," he said to them. "Excuse it."

They went out to the car, got in, and drove off.

"You did well, sister," the man said. "I wouldn't have thought you had it in y'."

He was holding the wheel firmly; when they came to the city limits, the car spurted. Their speed on the country highway was silent and she kept awake now for a while. White strips of fences blurred past them; the trees wheeled past in silence dripping light and vanishing. She was on her way. This humming of the motor was passage, another way to safety. As her eyelids fell, she heard faintly the thick clicking wheels of the train.

When she woke the next time, it was dawn. The man had his arms on the wheel and was driving fast.

"Awake?" he said.

"Yes."

"We're almost there. Recognize the scenery?"

They were crossing a long meadow.

"Yes," she said.

"You'll be home pretty soon now, sister."

She tried to realize that ahead of her was a great city, the city pictured in rotogravure, studied in maps, which was living, real, but which she had never seen. Refuge? Life? She held to the car—with a plunge that frightened her, they swept down into a tunnel. White walls flowed past her; at intervals there were uniformed policemen. "Ever been through the tunnel before?" the man said. "No." As the tunnel extended on gradually down and then gradually up, expectation began to tighten in her. Other cars ahead and behind roared evenly, undisturbed in this subterranean dawn. Atmosphere was sucked out around her, and sick at the pit of her stomach, she saw ahead a square of cold light. The car came up; converging down on her, in its unknown masses of setbacked buildings, was the city she had never seen. City—

"Where do you live?" the man said.

Quick. "East Eighteenth Street," she said. He turned the car into a narrow street, into an abrupt channel of buildings. They drove quickly on, block by block, weaving through traffic. City. Stopping finally at a cross-street, he said, "I haven't time to go across town with you. Have you some money?"

"No," she said.

He handed her a dollar bill. "Take the cross-town trolley," he said. "Or a taxi. Ride home in style, sister."

She started to refuse the money. "It's all right," he said. "You earned it."

15

SHE WAS alone on the street corner. Looking up she saw a sign which said 14TH STREET, SEVENTH AVENUE. She held the dollar bill folded up concealed in her hand. Money. From now on she knew that a new struggle would begin, to get money. A few people were passing, each face hard, purposive, with no look outward. Where were they going, the faces disjoined, unrelated, separating. The morning light was growing, and with it a massive acceleration of sound; taxis hurrying, trucks pounding by, and from under her feet came a subterranean murmur. Life underground. Life everywhere, solid miles of life. And she was unknown.

Was she safe now? A trolley came towards her, and as it went by, eastward, she saw a policeman at the street center directing traffic. Could he know? What about her appearance, the strange bundle she was carrying? Broadcast—radio, telephone, teletype—police reaching out. She had read stories in the newspapers, of cordons, nets. Did this one know? She turned around quickly; she must get out of sight. Across the street was a cafeteria, similar to the one where the man had stopped the night before. She almost ran to it.

Once inside, she felt safer. The smells of food, steaming smells from the counter. Somebody touched her arm and said, "Check," and looking in front of her she saw a metal box holding out a ticket. "Should I take this?" she said. "Yes." She took the ticket, a bell rang, and another ticket appeared. 5 10 15 20...the money she would have to pay. This was a world of money; freedom, food, existence was money. In her hand was money, the dollar bill the man had given her. She went slowly to the counter and looked at the signs, telling the price of food. Neatly lettered: Coffee 5¢, Cereals 10¢. She thought of the heavy china cups of coffee at the hospital. No sign, no price. Was money life? "What will you have, Miss?" "Oatmeal." The counterman dished up a bowl of oatmeal for her, expertly flung it in front of her, and held out his hand for her check. "Check?" She gave it to him and with the same vicious expertness, he punched it.

She went to a seat and ate. Money. She must get more money. It had been her plan, when she got to New York City, to pawn her ring. The ring her brother had given her; he would be helping her. Yet how could she— Gently she tried to take it off. It was large when it had first been given to her; now it had grown tight to the flesh. She pulled harder, trying to get it past the first joint, but it only pressed the skin into a fold. She became frightened. She twisted and pulled, hurting the flesh. She wet it with her tongue and pulled. Suddenly it came off, and like a part of herself, she saw it lying in her palm.

She finished her cereal and got up. At the cashier's window she gave her dollar bill with the check and received money. So many coins, so much freedom. Now she must go out into the streets again. Fear. But she could not remain here, she must go out, risk herself. She decided to hurry across the street and go across town, in the direction the man had indicated to her. Again the faces, pouring towards her, the buildings and the sound of life. She walked for a block seeing the city through her fear as an abstraction, like something seen in a mirror. But as she went under an El structure and started down another block, she remembered her need of finding a pawnshop and her fear suddenly left her. She looked for the symbol of the three gold globes, watching both sides of the street, examining every window and entranceway.

For several blocks she saw nothing that looked like a pawnshop and came to an opening in the streets. A sign on a restaurant window said UNION SQUARE. Near the curb a man was selling suitcases for twenty cents. "Here, ladies and gentlemen, is a perfect suitcase, strong built of imitation reinforced leather with metal corners it will withstand hard wear rain and weather is strong enough to—" A small crowd stood around him. She walked closer to see and decided she could get her clothes and small belongings into the suitcase if she packed them carefully. It would look better having it than a bundle—she pushed forward and paying her money, bought one.

She would have to find a place to pack it, where she would not be seen. She went down a side street and saw through a glass door some steps going up apparently to the second story of an office building. Unnoticed?—she went hurriedly inside and sitting on the steps, quickly transferred her belongings from the pillowcase to the suitcase, just fitting them in. She finally folded the pillowcase itself and jammed it in on top—I.H. the monogram of the hospital, I must get rid of that. She had just pushed shut the small suitcase and locked it, when she heard steps at the head of the stairs. She got up, put her jacket over her arm, and went out calmly into the street.

Now she must find a pawnshop. She went into a store and asked hesitantly if they knew where a pawnshop was. The manager, who spoke to her, looked at her oddly. "Yes, there is one a couple of blocks away. But—" "In which direction?" He told her. "Thank you," she said. When she came to the shop, she was surprised: there were no gold globes, and it was called not a pawnshop but a Loan Office. As she stood looking at it, she felt repelled by the air of secrecy, the closed and tightly curtained door. City respectability, hypocrisy. Yet her feeling changed—it would mean money, safety for her for a little while. She pushed open the curtained door and went inside.

The interior of the shop was dark and bare. Only on one side was a huge ornate pink and white vase, with two half-nude women on it in heavy relief, which stood on the counter. The walls were bleak and unwindowed. "What is it?" a man said who stood behind one of the counters.

"I want to pawn a ring," she said, holding out her ring. It was gold, with a small stone. She was sure it must be valuable, if only because her brother would have given her a good ring.

"Five dollars," the man said.

"It must be worth more than that!" she said.

"Yes, but that's all we can give you on it. Wait a minute."

The man took the ring into a small inner room, through the door of which she could see an open safe. He conferred with somebody, came back, and said, "Yes, that's all we can give you on it."

"All right," she said; there was nothing else for her to do.

"We have to figure on what we can get if we have to sell it," he said.

He laid the ring down on a green writing pad on the counter and taking out a ticket, picked up one of three worn black pens and began writing. The pen scratched loudly, stubbornly. "Name?" Harriet Demuth? No, she might be traced through the ring. She made up a name. "Address?" She made up an address. The pen scratched on. When the man was finished, he went back again into the little room and came out with a new five dollar bill which he snapped as he gave it to her.

She folded the bill in her hand and left.

16

A ROOM. She must find a room. Food, a room, the two simple things she must have. As she walked slowly along the street, light came and went on the pavement, unclearly shadowing buildings, or upward hitting the yellow tile of a chimney, dark walls. She thought, In this city, somewhere unknown, is my room. Through and beyond a wall level against the street ahead of her, she saw in blocks of light and shadow the room she had left. It faded into the solid city. It was gone. Now she would have a room in which to be secure, the hours undisturbed, her own.

Going from street to street slowly, she saw an occasional sign: FURNISHED ROOMS. Stopping in front of one building with grilled lower windows she went up to the entranceway and rang the bell. A woman opened the door.

"How much is a room?" she said.

"Ten dollars."

"A month?"

"No, a week." The woman looked at her with some surprise.

"Oh!" Hesitating— "You have nothing cheaper?"

"No. How much did you want to pay?"

"Three dollars."

"Three dollars! No, I have no room for three dollars and I don't think you'll find any around here. But if you go over towards Seventh Avenue, I think you might find something."

"Thank you."

She remembered the direction of Seventh Avenue and walked back to it. After trying without success in three or four places, she walked again towards the east. The sun was out clear, washing along the flat brick walls. Almost every house had a sign: ROOMS or FURNISHED ROOMS, and from the appearance of the buildings, she thought they must be cheaper. The ground floor entranceways, most of them, opened on long corridors, tunnels of pallid darkness—unshaven men stood in them, in one was a colored girl in a discolored dress leaning over a pail. The men watched passersby—with their inquiring look, she thought they must be landlords, ready to come out and accost anybody who looked like a prospective tenant. They embarrassed her, and rather than approach any of them, she went up some steps to a closed door and rang the bell.

A woman answered, large, foreign-looking.

"How much is your cheapest room?" she asked at once.

"Three dollars."

The woman spoke casually.

"May I see it?"

"Yes, come right in."

The room, she would see her room—now. The woman went forward down a dark hall; darkness unguessed from the street closed in on her. At the end of the hall was a staircase; known but unseen beyond it were a few heavy chairs under a low-turned gas jet. They started up the stairs, into the smell of decay. Off the second-story landing, in the half-light of a window she noticed an open closet with pails and inverted mops covered with floor cloths. "You take your bath on this floor," the woman said. "You'll have to tell me when you want a bath, so I can heat the water. Just now we have only a seventy-five gallon tank. In a month we'll put in a two hundred gallon tank. Then you'll have lots of hot water." Upward again a long flight of stairs. As they went up, the light increased until towards the top she saw a skylight. The building changed; the fourth story hallway was painted a dull orange, was cleaner looking, different from the lower floors. Around it in a row were a number of identical doors; the woman tried one, but was unable to open it. "It's locked," she said. She went through the room next to it to a back window and leaned out. "George!" she called.

A voice answered.

"I want the key to Patrick's room," she called. "I forgot it. It's too bad you have to wait," she said, coming back.

"I don't mind."

From below she soon heard heavy steps coming upward. A man appeared on the stairs who she thought must have weighed two hundred pounds; he had a head like a convict, round, bare, with shortcut hair that stood in a half-inch shock straight up from his forehead. His lips were protruding and yet not gross; his eyes were alive. He wore a dirty white suit.

"Here," he said.

He gave the woman the key. The woman said, "A man left this room a couple of days ago. We just got it ready this morning."

Now, the final moment— The key turned and at first she saw only a bright glare of green. It was the walls, which were of painted wood like the hallway and shone metallically. Hesitantly she stepped inside, carrying the suitcase. A small iron cot, a table with a rusty gas burner on it which was connected with a gas outlet by a rubber hose, a chair, a curtain to hang clothes behind. Two cheap chromo trays were nailed flat to the wall as a decoration and near the window on a shelf was a dirty tan plaster cast, apparently of the Winged Victory. A window filled the end of the small room, and beyond it were the rear walls of other buildings, the yards of this and neighboring houses utterly bare, filled with ashes.

"You want it?" the woman said.

"Yes."

"You pay the rent a week in advance. There's a twenty-five cent deposit on the key. You get that back when you leave."

She handed the woman the five dollar bill.

"Get change, George," the woman said. The man she called George went downstairs and came back with a dollar and seventy-five cents, the silver in small change. When she had counted out the change, she said, "Your name, please?"

"Harriet Demuth."

"Demut'?"

"Yes."

"I'm Mrs. Helios." They were standing in the room. "I think you'll be comfortable. This is my son George, he cleans the rooms." She stood waiting, as if she expected a word or two of discussion. Harriet said nothing. Saying again that she should be comfortable, the woman motioned to her son and went out.

She put her suitcase on a chair and went to the window. The sun. It came steadily through the window, making no shadows of bars. The key. It was to keep others out, not to keep her in. Whenever she wanted to, she could leave. She looked at the room, the green walls, the floor; she touched the white rough covers of her bed. Here, in this room, to stand, to move, to sleep. Here, perhaps, to live?

17

SHE SAT warming a piece of dry bread over the gas jet, which was turned low. It was early evening; two days had gone by since she had come here. Saturday. Except for going out a few minutes to the grocery store, she had stayed entirely in the room. A place of safety like the depth of the woods. Yet hers. Familiar, the sun turning upon it from darkness to darkness, wall to wall. Peace, familiarity. Her nightgown was behind the curtain at the head of her bed, she knew the creaking hardness of the bed, the sound of the floor. The exact number of steps from bedhead to window, from table to door. Gas jet—one of the first things she had done was to light it and tear the monogram from her hospital pillow-slip, burn it until it was completely destroyed. Later she threw away the pillowslip. Her room—during the two days, she had been disturbed only once. George had come up the morning before and knocked on the door; she knew his heavy step. When she asked what he wanted, he answered in an unclear voice and she said, "Never mind." She heard him say, "Clean bedding Tuesday," and go away. That had been all, of actual intrusion. But there were other things. She began to feel the life of the place. It was not simple. A complex life, in sound, sight, was flooding here—it was in slow, unjoined parts; it was hard to find its meaning. She turned the bread on the gas jet in front of her. There was a man living in the room next to her and there were other people on the floor. What were they? She had passed some of them; she had heard them speaking in the halls. This man next to her, in a room separated from hers only by a wooden partition, his steps, steps to

the window, the hall. There was something peculiar in his movements, he made no carefree sound, nothing unstrained, so that
she felt sure he was in trouble about something. Other sounds,
backward. Yet the room sheltered her and during the day there
was little movement. In the windows of a factory across from the
back of the house she could see women sitting at benches; she
could see their arms move, as if they were handling tools, but
could not see what they were doing. They were the only life during the day. She turned out the gas jet and began to eat the warm
bread. She wanted a bath. She had asked Mrs. Helios for a bath,
the first afternoon, and had enjoyed it in spite of its difficulty.
With no robe, she had to take her clean clothes down to the bathroom with her. A room half dark, the glazed window painted
over. She hung her clothes on a hook on the back of the door and
went to the tub. Lying on the bottom of it was the torn flap of a
box labeled REDUCING POWDER. She had no need for reducing
powder. If she could take a bath now, she could go to sleep.
Thinking of it, she heard a sound; somebody was singing in the
yard below. She went to the window and looked down. The backs
of the adjoining buildings and factories were dark; there was
night in the air. A man was walking out between the ash cans and
piles of junk looking for something. He was singing, the words
broken but the volume of his voice clear and strong.

She turned back to the room. As if from some shift or new
dimension, she felt fear. So many years now everything she had
seen had been the same—the same place, the same walls, buildings, corridors. The windows, the views from windows had been
the same, stationary, always there; the trees, the earth known,
never invading or changing. And within the buildings from year
to year the same rooms, smells, monotonously the same sounds,
words, whispers...

"*The cases in this ward* I want to see Dr. Stearns I want to see
Dr. Stearns one two three four one two three four who is that we
like to have visitors they use old silk stockings and underwear
they dye and cut *there are supposed to be only ten to one nurse but*

one two three four I want to see Dr. Stearns that's what I want to know if I did it or not"

She struggled, tearing at the sound. She might better die, or life might better threaten her nakedly, with no bulwarks, no separation. Anything was better, however harsh and threatening, than the words she heard in her mind.

The singing stopped. Since she had turned back to the room, it had been soft and she had hardly been sure she heard it.

18

It seemed she had been asleep only a short time when she was awakened by a knock on the door. The house was quiet, dead in sleep. Sleep came in a wave over the city. She listened. Again the knock, hesitant, as though the person knocking were undecided whether to waken her. She got out of bed, and not having a robe, put her jacket around her and opened the door.

A woman was standing outside, leaning against the door jamb. She was thin; her lips were painted. A gas jet burning low in the hall glistened in her vacant eyes. She had on a small hat and was holding a dark coat in her hand.

"Is he in?" she said, and nodded towards the next room door.

"No, I don't think so."

"No—he isn't in." She looked at the door, and went to it and knocked. "Dick!" she said. "Dick, are you there!"

There was no sound, the room was hollow with silence.

"Dick, for God's sake, Dick!"

There was a terrible directness in her voice, a terror of the empty room, dying out.

"No. No, he's gone." A flake of thin yellow hair fell down over her cheek like a child's. "I'm afraid."

Harriet held out her hand to her. "Don't leave me alone," the woman said. "Please, don't leave me alone!"

"Come in."

Guiding her, Harriet took her into her room. The woman sat on the bed. Gently she began to undress her, with careful hands. She took off her shoes, stockings, lifted her dress over her shoulders. She opened the bed and made her get in. The woman began to cry, her face pressed in the pillow, and gradually stopped. She got in beside her and held her as one would a child.

When she woke up early in the morning, the woman was asleep against her. The light of dawn was in the room, no sun. Life. The sounds she had heard from the next room, the man moving with his peculiar steps, trouble. It had been this; he had been deciding to leave her. The woman's face, she could see, was streaked with tears. She looked down at her body curved under the covers in sleep. Here was life against her, its breath touching, warming her arm. Slowly the sun came up and when it entered the room, the woman awoke.

"It's morning," she said. She sat up, put her long arms across her knees, and bent her head. "He's gone," she said. "I'll never see him again. Last night I was going to kill myself."

The sun became stronger, beating down over the buildings and factories. It was Sunday; there was no sound of work, of machines. The woman got out of bed and dressed. "What was it?" Harriet said. "I loved him, but I guess he never loved me." The sun on the green walls. The woman stood still, as though listening. She took her coat and hat and came to Harriet. "Thank you. You were good to me," she said.

Harriet heard her steps go down the stairs. The echo of the steps went on and on and she was alone.

19

TODAY she had decided to go out. Really out; her short walks to the store had been only from necessity. Going to the store, however, she had learned something which gave her courage. She had wondered if her clothes, the cut of her hair—the slight details that make up a correct appearance—were all right; if they betrayed her or if she could merge with the city. She had seen newspaper photographs at the hospital, she believed she looked all right, but it was a relief to know she did.

In the early afternoon when, with church over, people would be on the streets and she would be particularly unnoticed, she dressed and went downstairs. She met George in the lower hallway; he spoke to her in his blurred voice. She noticed he had on a clean white suit. She opened the front door and went quietly out.

When she was walking along the street, she found she was glad just to be outside of the house. She went under the Sixth Avenue El and walked on to Fifth Avenue; turning there, she went slowly south. Now she was asserting her freedom. Up and down both sides of the wide street, people walked, in a double file. Self-possessed, well-dressed, they walked confidently and for the most of them, in this moment there was no strange meaning in the street. There was just the sun, accepted and enjoyed.

As she approached Fourteenth Street, she saw a policeman standing on the corner talking to a man in ordinary dress. She had an impulse to turn back, but thought, No, from now on I must take this risk. Not quickening her steps, casually she walked by the policeman. He hardly glanced at her. "Listen, they tell

78

people J.P. Morgan is going to shine their shoes and John D. Rockefeller will hand them up to the chair!" "Naw, naw—"

Now she felt completely free. She began to enjoy what she saw. Ahead, becoming higher behind trees, was an arch. As she walked slowly along, beyond the fronts of buildings that she looked at curiously, she became more and more aware of the arch. It widened as she came nearer to it—the street seemed to end in it, and behind it there was a park. When she reached the arch, she walked through its shadow into the park.

In the park were rows of wooden benches with iron arms, along walks curving all around the flat park. Most of the benches were filled; children of every age played underfoot, loudly, running, ceaselessly in motion. There were few children at the hospital; she had played with none since she was a child herself. She suddenly wanted to be close to them, to be one of them. Their faces were like something lost.

She kneeled in a group of children only two or three years old. They were wearing sun suits, their dusted rosy limbs were round with just-left infancy. A little silence fell; one of the boys in the group held out a stick to her. "Break this, please," he said. She broke the stick and gave it back; automatically he started digging with it. The little sound of forgetfulness began again, voices rushed into syllables of childhood. A girl with a blue pail climbed on her knees and began to stare into her eyes. What is she looking at? Solemn, the stare was neither liking nor dislike, was not even inquiry. Understanding? But the eyes were shut with infancy.

One of the mothers came towards her.

"Sally seems to be fascinated by you," she said.

"Yes," she said. She stood up.

"Come back now," the mother said to the girl. The girl went away.

She too walked away.

There were a number of Italian children playing in the park, their faces harder, more independent than the other children's. She looked at all the children, but no longer hoped to come close to them. When she was tired, from walking in the paths of the park, she found a seat and sat down. The sun glittered on the points of railings.

20

SHE HAD gone to bed early and woke early, looking out at the gray dawn. It was Monday morning and today, as she had thought it over, she would start to look for work. Money. In a few days what money she had left would be gone; already it was less than a dollar. Food, this room. She was entirely dependent on money; without it she would soon reach the end of hope, of freedom. She stared at the green wall opposite her and began to think, to plan. She could do only the simplest kind of work, she realized, and she thought it was probably against her that she had no experience of anything, had never worked, and could offer no reference to former jobs. If they asked her, she thought, she would say she had just left school.

It would be important to dress very carefully. She had washed some of her clothes—stockings and underwear—and she had one clean dress left. She tried to clean the roughness of the leather on the toe of her right shoe, which still remained from her ride on the train. She could not do much with it. Except for this, though, she felt, when she was dressed, that she looked all right.

She ate, as usual, dry toasted bread for her breakfast and watched the day rising beyond the roofs of the buildings. It was the fourth morning since she had taken the room; she knew now how the sun came up, how its first thin line would fall against the green wall and, as she had noticed, touch the Winged Victory. It seemed slower than usual, and rather than wait, she went down, to meet it, into the opening of the street.

Outside, the air was clear. Walking along, she sucked it into her, like an odor. She went to a news dealer on the corner and bought a paper, putting it under her arm and walking on. In a store entranceway that was still locked, she stopped and opened the paper to the HELP WANTED—FEMALE section. The columns of fine print Steno-secty German-English dictation machine opers. with stock brokerage exp. on P. & S. work milliners first class forelady experienced handling operators corsets girdles brassieres brushmakers experienced on shaving brush knots—she looked up. It was useless, there was nothing. Nothing she could do, all of these jobs required experience. Also how could she get to the places advertised—she had no money for carfare, or as some of the jobs required, for telephone calls. The newspaper was a mistake, and because it cost two cents, a costly mistake; she must find some other way.

She walked on. She had no idea of what to do. She saw a doorway in which women were entering a building. She went in with them. One of them noticed her as she looked uncertainly around. "Who are you looking for?" the woman asked.

"Nobody," she said. "I'm looking for work."

"Oh, you want the employment office. Go down this corridor and inside the door is an elevator. Take it to the fifth floor. I don't think the office is open yet—maybe—"

She took the elevator and found the employment office. It was open, but nobody was there; windows and offices down the sides of the room were closed and blank. On rows of folding chairs in the middle of the room a few girls were already sitting. She took a seat near the front; soon a number of other girls came. "You seen the ad?" one girl said to another.

"Yeah."

When she had waited an hour, a door abruptly opened and a man came out with a cigar clenched between his teeth.

"You all here for the ad in the paper this morning?" he said.

There was a murmur, "Yes. Yes."

"Let's see, I haven't much time. Line up over there."

The girls crowded against a wall, those in the front seats taking positions at the head of the line. There were about fifty girls. "This is a one-day job, you know," he said. "Sale of coats. All we want is five girls to pick up coats after the sales-ladies. Now let's see. You and you and you and you and you. That's all. The rest of you can go. We have no more work."

The girls he had selected stood apart and the rest slowly left the room. "Gee, only five he wanted. Can yuh tie that!" Harriet followed the girls leaving the building. For a moment when the man was talking, she had thought he was going to choose her; his pointing finger had seemed to hesitate. "You—" But it had chosen another girl.

"Where y' going now?" The girls were talking, in a group breaking up on the sidewalk. She saw two of them walk away and decided to follow them; all they did was go to a subway.

Now what should she do? She tried in several restaurants, asking for a position as waitress "or whatever you have." They said no flatly or looked bored, as if many had asked the same question. In one place, the manager, an intelligent-looking man, said, "Have you ever worked as a waitress?"

"No," she said.

"Well, we can't break girls in. There are too many with experience looking for these jobs. In some of the small country hotels, maybe." Down the long vista of the restaurant she saw her face in a mirror. It seemed to show a change, the first change. She turned and walked slowly out. As she smelled the food at the counter, she realized she had been living for a week on very little food, poor food. Her strength was not the same as when she had left the hospital.

Outside was a tall office building and she decided to try that. She took an elevator to the fifth floor and began asking there from office to office—publishing firm, two garment firms, an agency for perfumes, ELLMAN & CO., other names on doors, other businesses. Always she was finally told, "No, nobody is wanted." She tried two other floors, and each time that she was turned away, felt less hope. The day was going; it seemed to rush towards the evening. Already it was noon.

"I'm looking for work."

"Well, this is only the sales office; we don't need anybody. But I think they're taking on some girls at the factory. I'll give you the address of that if you want."

"Yes, I do."

The clerk wrote an address on a slip of paper and gave it to her. She asked how to get to the factory. The clerk gave her directions— "It's about sixteen blocks."

Her hope, some of her strength returned. She walked; she felt, as she walked, an ache growing down her thighs. At the factory, a wooden building, she hesitated looking for the right entrance. When she went in, she saw a bare room divided by a railing behind which several girls were working at typewriters. She went to one of the girls nearest the railing who seemed to be in charge.

"I was told by the sales office that you were taking on some help. I'd like to apply."

"I don't think we're hiring anybody now, but see Mr. Masler in the office there." The girl pointed. She went into a small office and saw a man sitting at a desk.

"I want to apply for work," she said. "I was told by the sales office you were hiring some help."

"Well, we took a few girls this morning, but we're all filled up now." He looked at her, changed his tone. "However, we might have something, if— Are you living at home?"

"No."

"You're living alone?"

"Yes."

He looked at her speculatively. "Would you—uh, would you appreciate a favor?"

"How do you mean?"

He explained.

She turned and walked rapidly out of the office, through the bare room beyond. The typewriters clicked for a moment, pushing her to the street.

Sun. She was out now, outside, in the air. A word he had used, she tried to wipe it from her mind. She felt the same as when her leg had been caught under the train. Safe, yet knowing the power of something to hurt. It was harder than she had thought.

She needed to rest, to get strength. She saw a small restaurant—COFFEE POT—and went inside. Workmen, food. She got a bowl of soup. As she ate, as the warm strengthening soup and bread she ordered began to fill her, she looked out at the street. The sun shone on some iron shutters, masonry. Was there work, hope, anywhere, off any of these streets? She must go on looking. It was not a matter of courage; it was the only way to keep what she wanted.

As she went out into the street again, the sun hit her. Other factories? She tried in building after building. Going into buildings, the continual hope of the street. Yet NO HELP WANTED signs. Refusal, waiting, refusal. She became irritated with these streets of generally low, often vacant, time-wracked buildings. Hope died in them. She finally turned and went back to the office building area.

Office to office; the weight of the afternoon grew in her. She knew that the pain across her thighs, her shoulders, the growing physical difficulty of continuing, of opening doors, asking, going out, showed in her face. Yet since she must, she kept on.

At six o'clock, she felt faint. Doors swung against her mind, mouths moved "nothing nothing" corridors elevators sprang up down, NO HELP, "work?" It was only by holding nothingness back in her that she walked to her rooming house and climbed up to her room.

21

HER EYES opened the next morning when it was so dark she could hardly tell it was day. A dull beat of rain sounded on the roof overhead, and in a faint sound outside the window reiterated ceaselessly. She would be unable to look for work today. Her head fell back, the imprisoning and vacant sound pleasing her. This is rain, that falls on the hospital roof, weaving among the black porches whispers, the repetitive sound of the world.

When she got up, she felt a little cold, and lighted the gas burner. It bleakly hissed and warmed the room. She dressed, feeling listless, and went to the window and looked out on the gray film of rain. Several times she put her hands to her ears and quickly took them away. The rain cried ah, ah, speaking to her. Beyond today and tomorrow, some moment of time from which there would be no return.

In the middle of the morning there was a knock on the door.

"Come in," she said.

George came in holding clean sheets and a pillowcase. "Here's your clean bedding," he said. "Throw the old ones outside the door."

"All right."

He hesitated, holding the bedding over his arm. Huge, impersonal, lonely. She saw his loneliness—behind his jowls, his eyes; the life of such men, she thought, of men gross and brutal, must be frightening. "The rain," he said in a deep voice. "What?" He said that it was like the Amazon; it made the steam, the "fever." "Hot there," he said. From sentences disjointed, hard to follow, she began to understand that he had been in the rubber trade. He talked of death; it was a place where men always died. "Five, five while I was there." Rubber, "the gum." An assistant, a Scotchman. In five minutes, she could never see it clearly, but the assistant too had died "in his arms." His death had broken George; soon he had himself sickened and natives had rowed him down to Para. "The natives thought I was God," he said. "Why?" "I did something—" They always put sand in the center of their balls of rubber; it was to make them weigh more. He stamped a number on each ball; when it was sent down the river, purified, he had an account sent back of the weight of sand. He called the natives in, one by one—deducted so much from their accounts, ten pounds, twenty pounds. "How long were you there?" "Oh, three four years." He smiled. "I guess I got children down there." His eyes changed, looking out at the rain. Loneliness? Suddenly they were both silent, and the rain droned its continual sound. He laid the clean bedding on the bottom of the bed and went out, closing the door. Human, living; she looked at the wet, ash-strewn earth streaked with lines of water. The day reached ahead of her monotonous with sound.

Towards noon, she left the room and went downstairs, into the depth of the house. Now she had lost the rain, everything but darkness. In the bottom hall in the light of the gas jet, she saw the same phantasmal furniture. She had wanted to ask for a bath, but she could not break this silence. She started up again, floor by floor. As she neared the top, the rain gradually sounded again, hitting the upper floor skylight. She saw a newspaper behind the top newel post and took it into her room with her. The green walls had an undersea look. She sat near the window to read; nothing interested her until she came to a headline: SUBWAY "HOME" TO 75,000 GIRLS. "'Their nights are spent riding in the subways. I have heard them say often, "If you know how to go uptown, downtown, and across town, you can ride all night for a nickel."'"

Knotted in her handkerchief on the table were a few coins; among them was a nickel.

She put the paper down and looked out the window. Even

through the intervening rain, she could see in the factory windows the women working, their bare arms repeatedly making the same movements. Work. If she only had work like them, if she only understood their movements, how to handle the tools. She watched them for a long time, the white faces behind the windows, until the afternoon darkened and they became invisible.

She lit her light and ate supper. She saw George's cropped hair and heavy lips. She had talked to him, there had been knowledge of death between them. When she finished eating, she sat again at the window. Lights from other buildings rayed out in the rain; the dark grew complete.

She remembered now a day of her childhood which she had once or twice remembered before. Her father had been fond of walking and as they lived on the edge of town, he would go out often into the country. Sometimes he took her with him; she enjoyed looking at the places they passed, country fields and buildings. One day in late fall after a rain he had set out with her and they went along a road they had not taken before. The day was completely overcast and cold; the trees were leafless. Because of the cold, of something in the air, she began shivering—as a child she had been inclined to shiver. Her father saw it and began to walk faster. She still shivered, the cold frightened her. She clenched her hands and drew them into her coat to escape; her spine stiffened and she kept shivering noticeably. "Stop that," her father said—"You're thinking too much about the cold. Let yourself go." They continued walking, in this awkward way. The gray wet earth stretched between her and the horizon. Soon she was in pain from the shivering. Her father, knowing nothing else to do, turned back. When they reached home, even the warmth of the house failed to stop her shivering and suddenly she felt weak and lay down on the bed in her bedroom. "Mother!" she called. When her mother came, she said, "Something's the matter with me"; the shivering shook the bed. It went on and on and she felt that nothing would stop it, that she was going to die. After about two hours it stopped.

2 2

THE SUN was out. Sitting eating the last of her food she had kept for that morning, she looked at the Winged Victory. A stationary wind was blowing the draperies; the headless body was like the flow of dawn. Yesterday the same as Monday. "I'm sorry, we have nothing." The wings had beaten, yet—NO HELP WANTED posted behind walls, on turned foreheads.

She got up and packed her small suitcase. She had to leave, this morning. The bed unmade had the print of her body in it; the sun was in the room. Unless she found work today, this was the only room she would ever have; it had become a part of her. She knew it all, had it fixed in her memory. Each part of the room was hers now.

She looked at the bed, thinking of the woman who had slept in it, the few hours of night and morning when the woman had been with her, when she had felt her breath against her. She thought of the silence of the room, the sight of the women working in the factory. Alive. The man singing, looking for something among the ashes—Threat. Acceptance. It had been good. Even if she found no work today and the last feared moment came, she was satisfied; these hours would have existed. She turned, opened the door of the room, and closed it behind her.

"You're leaving?" George said, as she met him in the lower hall.

"Yes, I'd like the deposit back on my key."

He looked at her puzzled. "What's the trouble?" he said, in his indistinct voice. "Isn't everything all right?"

"Yes, but I have to go."

He was going to say something more, but seeing her distressed face, remained silent. He went past the stuffed furniture into the dark; after a minute he came back with his mother.

"You're leaving?" she said.

"Yes."

"That's too bad. Maybe I could let you have the room for less."

"No, I'm sorry. I have to leave."

"There's nothing wrong, you're sure? If it's the bath, I'll have the new tank put in in two weeks."

"No," she said desperately, "I just have to go."

Mrs. Helios' face changed; it was as if at the same moment she and her son recognized something. "Oh, all right then," she said.

"Here's the key."

"You want a quarter." She got a coin from her apron pocket and gave it to her. They hesitated. "If you come back some time, we'll be glad to have you," the woman said.

She said good-by and left.

At the corner of Sixth Avenue, she tied the quarter she had received in her handkerchief. It was the last money she had. The day, with its strange finality, was ahead of her. She gripped the money in her hand until the skin was white over her knuckles.

It would be better if she had no suitcase when she went to look for work. She walked towards the office district, and stopping at a little clothing shop, asked the girl behind the counter if she could leave her suitcase there until six o'clock. The girl hesitated as if estimating the size of the suitcase, and then said yes. "We close at six," she said.

Now summoning all her strength, she started again to look for work. It was like the other days, the same doors, faces, refusals. When she was told, "No, nothing," she offered to work for just enough to live on. One man in a small establishment said, "We get girls for less." As the day went on, her strength lessened; she could feel it leaving her. It was more than tiredness; she had the apprehension of collapse. She needed food . . .

At six o'clock, she went back for her suitcase. She walked

slowly. In the neighborhood of the store she had seen a small park and when she had her suitcase, she went directly there to sit on the benches. As she sat, facing the night, for the first time she felt afraid. When she was rested, she went to a nearby restaurant and ate. She had spent ten cents for lunch. She spent ten cents now. She knotted the remaining nickel into her handkerchief. After she had eaten, she went again to the park and sat down. She waited until after dark, in complete apathy, watching the buildings turn to shadow and lighted windows appear; at last she got to her feet and carrying her suitcase, walked slowly to the streets.

For two hours more she tried to find work. Wherever there were lights, she tried. She left her suitcase in hallways, went quickly in and came quickly out. Those who were there usually told her to come the next day or said, "No, nothing." At about eleven o'clock she could go no farther.

It was now deep night. The street she was on was dirty, littered with papers. Children on several corners were making fires with waste paper and boards in the gutters; the flames flickered on their faces. She pressed the nickel in her hand; "75,000 girls." As a man approached her, she said, "How do you get to the subway?" "Two blocks ahead." She walked in the direction he had pointed, but more slowly. Now the night had changed, for she was leaving it. She looked as if for the first time seeing what was around her; the sides of buildings in the dark, doorways, the store fronts. Across the street was the rear of a school, with fire escapes going up it, thin and black against the brick. She saw clearly, her eyes opened for the first time, and came slowly to the light burning beside the subway entrance. For a few moments she stood looking down, and suddenly heard a roaring sound grow and die away below ground. Overhead, over the shadowy buildings, was the sky. Staring at it, she began to go, step by step, down into the earth.

PART TWO

I

SHE STOOD on the platform watching the train head approaching. This was what the newspaper said, "home." Tunnel, night opening to deeper night. "Across town" other girls at least knew the subway, this train, the long platform broken with girder-blunted light. Screech, the doors began to open, people moved on. Holding her suitcase, knowing she must, she followed, beginning the necessary journey that must keep her until dawn. With a jerk the train swung forward, racket of wheels, chains, indistinct. With her suitcase under her legs she sat straight, trying to see, to attach herself to the train. At least she was sitting down. She forgot hunger. A few stations and the train began slowly to fill. Two girls sat down opposite her, her own age, she thought— They held pocketbooks in their laps; one of the pocketbooks was black, the other of some kind of alligator skin. She kept staring at the pocketbooks and the hands holding them. She could see the confidence drawn inward from the hands through the pocket-book straps. She tried to look away. After a few stations the girls got up and left the train.—Now the silence roared, continuing unchanged under the change of gear. Forward, wheels, chains, shift of curve, of light. At a long station, many well-dressed men and women got on, the men with dark coats and silk hats and the women with gold or silvertinsel heel-dragging dresses. One of these women had a blue ribbon tied in a bow at the neck of her dress; she untied it and retied it again. The walls beyond the windows were black. She looked down, hunger. Gradually the men and women left the train and she wondered if it were time to change. She had to change, the paper said. A map of the subway system was posted in a window by the middle door. Hanging to a porcelain strap she looked at it, deciphering the difficult lines, stations. The train was going uptown, they were in the Hundreds. She saw two lines crossed at MOTT AVENUE: she held her suitcase against her knee. "Where do you wanna go?" a man asked her. "Mott Avenue." "That's three stations furder on." She sat down, the walls flowing, the passage of a black sky, thunder. One. Again. Two. Again. MOTT AVENUE; she got up and left the train. Stepping on the solid platform she felt a moment of nausea, her body converging towards her throat. She looked at signs, walking to steps to other steps. Here the long avenue of lights girderpost-blunted, now the dark return of rails. Freedom, "home"; a train roared in. She was sitting again with her suitcase under her legs, the walls drawing the vacuum the extended night. It would be a long way now, surely it would be a long way to the station where she would change again. A new voice— "Latest pehpehs latest pehpehs"—coming, louder, passing, the boy leaving papers spread out in front of her. Two men beside her and four opposite had them; the front and back showed BOY KILLER —pictures of the boy, attorneys, witnesses, of the boy's mother, the mother of the girl he had murdered, swaying, turned, raised BOY KILLER GETS CHAIR. She looked, on the back of a paper opposite her, at the picture of the electric chair. THE CHAIR. BOY KILLER—FATAL CAR CRASH ENDS BALM SUIT. She looked down. From time to time she was overconscious of the train's sound; she kept listening to it, hearing it. A highpitched horn would sound warningly, they would come into a station, and while still, she noticed the train was not silent but kept up a rhythmic beat. Moan, brakes, rapid change to speed. Suddenly she was not hearing it, it faded into the silence of faces and the concentric black walls. In front of her eyes the blackness began to spread, reaching tentatively towards her and enclosing her. Onward, the melodic speed screeching; she swayed. Suddenly— How far had the train gone? She looked at the station they were leaving and went to the map again, terror in her. They were in Brooklyn! She stood at the door and at the next station got out. "How do you get to New York?" she asked. "Manhattan train, over there." The dark empty station, steps, a second platform. This time in walking she felt the lethargy deeper, her limbs her body moving against continual obstruction. She could hardly hold the suitcase, or stand to wait. The train came in; she got on awkwardly and sat down. Suddenly she felt uncontrollably sleepy. Her eyes closed; her body slumped against a car card at the end of the car. At each station she roused up, afraid to give in entirely to sleep, seeing on beyond each station MOTT AVENUE where she must get off. There were fewer people in the car now. At the end of the seats, men had taken positions where they could put their legs up. Heads were sunken on breasts. Now in this deep shadow, faces changed less often; a look she had noticed of mutual fear and recognition increased. She turned from the eyes of the men that even in sleep looked at her. On the car card against which her shoulder leaned somebody had scrawled THE ENTIRE PER-LEECE DEPT. IS A DOPE. She stared at it and unbelievingly saw Mott Avenue appear beyond the windows. Again lethargy drawing against her body. She reached the downtown side and saw a clock. Quarter of one. The long steps and the same platform long, deserted now; gray lines of the posts darker. Again the train took her. The roar and humming of the train beat fiercely now, on the edge of death. Her head sagged; it was almost impossible for her to look up at each station. Sleep, the mercy of nothingness even here— If there were somewhere to sleep. Some still place. Desperately, she got out at a station and determined to find a place to sleep. She came slowly up the steps to the first upper level. Near her was a closed newsstand and beyond it an open concourse leading to gates, turnstiles, railings. She walked across the open space. Men with drugged eyes passed her. All at once she stopped; she saw a number of men sleeping in shoeshining chairs. The chairs were on daises; each man slept with his head back and his closed eyes staring into an electric light hanging above him. Between

the chairs were large signs, SHINE 5¢. The men slept motion-
lessly; seeing them sleeping there under the hard light, publicly,
where all who passed could see them, she hurriedly turned and
went back to the platform she had left. Here she stood weakly, her
body toppling forward or backward at the least change of balance. Men around her sat on steps, half-sat on the lower rung of
the guard rails, squatted on the base of several penny weighing
machines. On a bench a woman and five men sat, motionless,
with their eyes tightly closed. When the train came, these people
got up and the train carried them and her away. She watched station by station and somewhere downtown changed and came uptown again. Her mouth was dry, her tongue thick. Whenever she
opened her eyes, the light burned them like an acid. She felt pain
in her forehead. Her breath came deeper and deeper, as if she were
fighting for every breath. Roar, whir, beat of motors poured upon
her—her strength thinned against it; she could endure it no longer. She got up. She held on to an enamel railing and waited until
the train came into a station. Then, as the door opened, she staggered out. A grinding click, a receding sound; she was alone in
silence.

2

As she came up the steps, around the railing out of the subway exit, she saw directly facing her the neon light of an all-night cafeteria. Red. Behind her a taxi whined towards the curb, slowed, and its red light echoed in her forehead. Gone, "O God God" she turned towards the cafeteria window, staring through the clear glass. Quiet. She went through the door, taking a check, and sat down in a chair. Underground. It was roaring on, the sound dying out. Red, corridors. "You must drink it it will make you sleep"

Somebody was shaking her shoulder. "You have to buy something, Miss. You know—"

She looked up. "I can't," she said.

"You'll have to leave, then."

At a nearby table a man was sitting. She saw him and her eyes gradually cleared. He had on a gray workingman's shirt, open at the collar; the shirt was not too clean. Sweat had given the shirt the shape of his shoulders which were strong-looking. From the open collar she could see how his neck began, thick, strong. The oval of his head was outlined by black hair and a two-day growth of dark beard. Through the beard, she could see the cast of his features; they were hard, yet young. His eyes were kind; they seemed to have understanding. They looked at each other in silence, waiting. Then—

"Come on, get going."

The man got up and came over.

"What's the trouble?" he said.

A man, evidently the night manager of the cafeteria, said, "She isn't buying anything." "Let her alone," he said. "I'll get her something." The manager hesitated and then walked away.

"Do you want coffee?" the man said.

She nodded. He went to the counter and came back with a steaming cup of coffee. The manager came back. "Never mind paying for it," he said.

"I'll pay for it," the man said.

He put the cup of coffee by her hand. She leaned over it—the steam, acrid familiar smell. She drank it slowly; it warmed her stomach.

"Do you want anything to eat?" he said.

"No," she said. She felt no hunger.

His hands rested on the table; she saw that they were large and calloused. "What's the trouble?" he said.

"Nothing. I was riding the subway and—I couldn't go on any longer."

"You don't know anybody here?"

"No."

"You can come to my place for the night, if you want to."

"All right," she said.

"You're sure you don't want something to eat?"

"No."

They went out together, into the dark. Their steps sounded against the vacant quiet of the street. They walked several blocks and turned into another street, darker, the sky overhead meeting gray white curtains, windows empty with sleep. Like intruders, they walked between the last echoing silence of the night. Coming to a grated metal gate beside a large building like a stable, the man stopped, opened the gate, and motioned her inside, into a passageway. Slit of sky. She heard the gate swinging to behind them, clanging. They walked forward, she ahead of him, down a narrow walk between two buildings and came out into a bare courtyard paved with broken cement. In front of them was a three-story house ribbed with clapboards; it was all she saw. Inside, a staircase, near which a light was burning. Up. At the second landing, the man took a key out of his pocket and opened a door. She went in ahead of him, moonlight shone in two windows, disappeared as he switched on a light. A room; against a wall there was a bed.

The man put her suitcase down; she pulled off her hat.

"I'll leave you for a while," he said. He went out and closed the door behind him.

3

THE NEXT morning when she woke up, she felt that she was alone. Silence, in the room, in the building. Blur of hair. She tried to think; How had it happened? She lay unmoving and at last sat up, the covers slipping to her knees. The room was empty; it faced east, there was late morning sun in it. Opposite the bed was a large armchair and doubled over the top of it was a thin cushion indented in the middle. Then he had slept there. Underground, men on the daises—The room's silence was broken only by the sound of the city and by the momentary rumble of horses' hooves; the building in front was evidently a stable. She slowly got out of bed; she stood fastening the side of her dress when she saw a note. In pencil he had written: "Please stay till I get back tonight. Want to talk. There's food in the kitchen." Under the note was the key of the room. She looked at the armchair and its indented cushion again. Now she heard the sound of a train; it became a clock, faint. Eleven o'clock. An open door, darkness. She went into the kitchen which had no windows and was so dark she had to find an electric light and turn it on. There was a sink with one faucet, of cold water. She rinsed and rubbed her hands and rubbed water on her face. Feeling better, she looked around and saw a breakfast laid out for her: an orange, dry cereal, milk, bread. She picked up the globe of the orange...

When she had eaten, she started looking for a bathroom. She could find none, only a small storeroom. Taking the room key, she went out into the hall. Another door; locked. The stairs. On the landing below, two steps led up to a short passageway towards the back of the house. Smell of dried paint, rot; all the doors here were locked except one, into a room entirely dark in which a gas flame burned with a hissing sound. Toilet. She tried to close the door behind her. No knob either outside or inside; it could only be fastened by a small chain with a ring on the end which fitted over a nail. No washbowl, no bathtub. The toilet paper was a pile of small square tissues in a cigar box.

When she had returned to the room, she looked at it again. There were a few books on a table: the Bible, *The Pilgrim's Progress*, *Machine Shop Practice*. In *The Pilgrim's Progress*, which she opened, she saw an inscription: To my son John on his eleventh birthday. She thought, His name is John. She took up the *Machine Shop Practice*. "An 18 inch lathe may have any length bed, but usually not exceeding 20 feet"; turned to another page, "but the best method is to mount the piece of work that is to be turned (or a piece of stock the same length) between the centers, using a dog as in a turning operation. At the end of the work by the headstock, take a narrow cut to a depth of a few thousandths of an inch. At this depth and without touching—" looked further, pictures of lathes, "milling machines," "drills." She put the book down. She went and looked out of the window. The courtyard was filled with sun, cut by a short shadow of the stable. From somewhere in the distance she heard the sound of a blacksmith's hammer; nearer, children were shouting. Beyond this, all the hollow sound of the city, automobile motors rising and falling, a noise of horns, voices— The sun, coming through the window, touched her hotly; sweat formed on her skin and slowly cooled.

What should she do? The hours of the day began to pass over her, the ticking clock, Think. The building in silence. Once she heard a dog bark upstairs; once she heard steps, but it was completely quiet. Again the clock, a decision? What should she do? "To talk" "to talk," no, not to give him knowledge, not to see death again. His eyes. Better to go now. For could he help her? How could she expect him to help her? His note. What could she do if she left? Another night perhaps and what then— There was no way. "Want to talk..." Her thoughts pried uselessly, caged, and she looked again at his note. His handwriting was strong; she grasped at any strength. Something would happen; even when there was no hope, something sometimes happened. The door at the hospital... She looked at the clock, Think. But thought would do no good. All that she had now was the knowledge of a face she believed she could trust. But was it trust or need? She went again to the window and stood looking for a long time at the movement of shadow. She had had years of practice in watching time, in the patience of waiting. The shade of the stable shrank and disappeared; the building she was in began to lengthen itself in the court. When would he come and what would she say and how would it end? She would not lie; she would withhold but not lie. The lies she had told in coming to New York had not mattered but this would matter. She must be honest with him. And yet, how could she be honest? Her thoughts returned trapped to the morning; the palms of her hands became moist. Better to go. She turned back to the room and suddenly felt weak. She heard the roar of the train underground; beyond it? The clock—

When he entered the building and she heard his steps up the stairs, steady, from floor to floor, it was too late. A tired sound in his tread, the slow steps of a man who is tired. The door, she had left it unlocked. She stood watching it; there echoed in her another moment of listening, of waiting. No key, she had the key. She looked down; when she looked up, he was standing in front of her.

"You're here," he said.

"Yes, I'm here."

"I'm glad. How do you feel, rested?"

"Yes, I'm rested."

After a moment he said, "I've tried to think, what to do. You said you didn't know anybody here in town; is that right?"

"Yes."

"Your father and mother, are they living?"

"Yes."

"Well, I have a little money; I'll help you get back to them."

She said, "I can't go back to them."

"Why not?"

"I—I can't."

"Why not?"

"Please—"

"But what are you going to do?"

"I don't know." She stared at him.

"I don't understand—"

Desperately she said, "I can't tell you. You'd understand if I did. But I can't; can't you believe me?" He said nothing. "Can't you see? Do I have to tell you?"

He still said nothing.

"All right," she said. "I'll go."

"No, wait." He blocked the door. "Don't go," he said.

4

SHE WAS sitting in the kitchen, while he got something ready to eat. She looked at him as he moved about under the harsh light. He did not look like the doctors or orderlies she had known at the hospital, but like the men who worked on the grounds. His face had marks of exposure and work, and there was something else about it. Understanding, shadow? His hair, she saw now, was not as dark as her own. His shoulders, although strong, appeared a little stooped; she had the impression that they were stooped not from bending over something but from crouching. His eyes— The same as the night before, they looked kind; she understood how he had helped her.

They ate and afterward she washed the dishes. He let her do it; it was the first work she had done since she left the hospital. She enjoyed the feeling of it. When she was finished, they went in the other room again. The courtyard was light, but although the sun had not yet set, twilight had come into the room. The man lay down on the bed and she sat down in the armchair. In the half dark, some of the tiredness left his face; he stared at the ceiling.

"What's your name?" he said.

"Harriet Demuth?"

"Demuth?"

"Yes." She spelled it for him.

"It's nice. What is it, German?"

"I don't know—I don't know much about my family."

He was quiet, as though he had forgotten her.

She said, "I thought in a city, like New York—I could find work."

"Yes—"

"I still want to look for work."

"Tomorrow is Saturday. Why don't you rest tomorrow and Sunday and if you want to, look for work Monday?"

"All right."

Through the open windows twilight poured, blurring, spreading darkness in the room. Evening sounds of the city—over houses, walls—came in with the dark. After a few moments she heard somewhere in a nearby building a phonograph beginning to play—a jazz record, a circular monotonous beat; when the needle swerved off the inside, the house's silence became deeper. The man lay prostrate, unmoving; she could not see him clearly; dark covered everything. Grief, from the record, fell along her mind; she thought of the distant room where Miss Cummings still was.

5

HE PUT some blankets on the floor that night to sleep. In the morning he left before she got up, but she was awake and spoke to him. "We need some coffee, I think some butter," he said. "You might buy them, and look around and see if there's anything else we need." He took a five dollar bill from his pocket and put it on the table. In the growing light of dawn she had looked at the green bill. She was still looking at it after he had gone.

The sun slowly came into the room, slanting along the wall near the bed. Disorder, she noticed now that the room was dirty. The rooms at the hospital were kept thoroughly cleaned and straightened. It was from living alone: men lost the instinct of order, they could no longer see. She got up and went into the kitchen; she noticed that the kitchen too was dirty, it needed a thorough cleaning. The dishes were kept on a shelf running around two sides of the room. She ran her finger over it; it was black. When she had eaten and finished washing the dishes, she started to clean the shelf, but saw that if she were to get it really clean, she would have to have scouring powder and would have to go to the store.

The five dollar bill was still on the table. A week of life; she pressed it tightly in her palm. Spend only a little. She looked out at the sun, towards the street which she had seen before only when it was dark and empty. Sounds of the day before, of children, shouts, closeness, loudening and dying. She felt a particular excitement, her senses alert. She took the key of the room and going out, locked the door carefully behind her.

Dark, the smell of stairs. She began to notice the stairs as she had not the day before. She leaned and looked down the dark stairwell. These stairs were not solid; their treads sagged, the staircase was pegged to the walls with iron rods at each landing. The house was old. She went down and when she came into the light of the lower open house door, she looked around her. She saw only a bare hallway; on one side was a large metal barrel with a warped cover, on the other a table on which were several letters—evidently this was where mail was left for those in the house. Except for this, the hall was vacant; scribbled on the plaster were a few names: "DIDOMENICO 2nd" "LICORA—"

She went out, crossed the courtyard, and going down the narrow passageway, came to the gate. It had a narrow grating, bands of heavy overlapping metal. Through it she saw a width of pavement, curbs, and the open house door of a house opposite. Sitting on the steps of this house was a little Italian girl. She slowly pulled open the gate; it swung to with a metallic clang behind her.

As she looked up and down the street, what she first noticed was the children—girls with short dresses blowing, boys with flesh in tears of their shirts or overalls; even infants were sitting on the sidewalk. She liked them. A few mothers shouted, but the children lived in their own kingdom; they heard nothing and their voices were concerned only with their own life. The buildings split above; bleak, worn, weak. There were puddles along the broken sidewalks; cobbles broke the sidewalks with entrances into rear yards or into open, steaming laundries. But beyond and over everything was the cry and life of the children; it was this child sound, distant and separate, rising and falling, that she had heard the day before.

Looking at everything, walking slowly, she came to a cross-street. Here there were pushcarts of vegetables and fruit, on both sides of the street. She had never seen pushcarts and stopped to look at them curiously. About a block away, on the other side, there was a church, rising with cold, sooty stone into the air. In this street she saw fewer children; shawled women picked their way along, talking and handling; salesmen arranged their wares. In shops life flowed around windows, showcases, poles, steps.

She found a small Italian grocery shop and bought the few things she needed. At another store she bought a cheap floorcloth; she had spent seventy cents, it seemed a great deal and she held her change carefully. She returned through the streets, the faces, the cries of the children to the gate. When she had entered and come again to the courtyard, for the first time she looked at the front of the house in sun. Forenoon heat; it seemed flat, gray, without color; the windows had worn frames and dusty panes. There was nothing green here, no grass, and yet the house was withdrawn from the street, like houses of small towns—beyond the courtyard. It had comparative quiet, too—no children lived in it; the people in it, men for the most part, were workers. At least they were gone in the daytime.

She went slowly up the stairs, smelling sallow plaster, feeling the uncertain sag of the treads towards the center. When she was on the stairs, the house seemed weak and almost about to collapse, but when she was in the room, it seemed strong again.

6

SHE HAD put away the things she had bought and started to work. She cleared off the shelf around the kitchen and heating some water, scoured it thoroughly. When she had finished the shelf, she looked around to see what to do next.

The floor. She found an old broom in a little closet in the kitchen, and swept the worst of the dirt up. When it was in a pile, she needed a dust pan to take it up but could find none. She took the piece of wrapping paper from the grocery bundle and swept it on to that. Now, she thought, water for the floors.

Two floors had to be cleaned, the kitchen and the other room. She heated more water and filled a large pan she found in the oven. Getting down on her hands and knees, she wet the new floorcloth and rubbed. Her thick hair fell across her cheeks, darkly swaying and shadowing her eyes. She felt the strength and balance of her body, pressing forward, the whole back pivoted by one arm to the other that moved with the cloth. In this way millions of women scrubbed. The soap bubbled out over the floor, dark water ran in little spurts ahead of the cloth. In the hospital, blank-faced women had scrubbed all the floors, patients doing what they could for themselves. They worked in silence; she had passed them in corridors and on stairs and there was no life in their eyes. But their movements were sure, they carried in their bodies the knowledge that generations of women and their own experience had given them. Their lowered heads, gathered skirts, the pails of water they changed proved their identity with all womanhood. Her thought went beyond them to her mother. Her mother too she saw on her knees beside a pail, her arm moving—her mother had had to scrub floors; there had never been a servant in the house. She saw her working; she saw herself too working, feeling it along her back, her arm, as her mother had. The wet, cleaned space of floor grew—she felt it clean; she looked at it widening beyond her with satisfaction.

When she had finished, she felt tired. She rested, and a languor came over her that she had not known in many years. She hardly moved. The sun shone on the clean floor; the wood had a fresh soapy clean odor. She lay resting until after the sun had left the room; then she got up and went in the kitchen and made herself a lunch.

During the afternoon, as she felt rested, she cleaned the kitchen sink. Its enamel was badly stained; she had to clean it inch by inch and it took her a long time. When she finished and went into the other room again, she was surprised to find it was nearly dark. She looked at the clock and thought, Soon he will be coming, and went to the window to watch. Outside the sun was still shining on the walls of buildings, and higher up the day was full of light. But in this room, as she had noticed the day before, the dark came early—the light the windows let in, without the sunlight, was not enough. As she watched, two Italians in working clothes came through the courtyard and entered the building. She heard one go into a downstairs room. The other went up to the floor above and she heard the dog barking she had heard in the morning.

At last she heard the gate and it was he, coming in, not looking tired now as he had the night before, and yet walking slowly. He crossed the court; behind him a slight thunder of horses' hooves rose, as if a horse nervous from the day's work were being roughly driven into the stable. Silence; he was coming up the stairs. She did not leave the window. He opened the door and came in, with an immediate quick look to find her. "Hello," he said, and threw his cap on the table. At first he noticed nothing, and then she saw his nostrils quiver. He had smelled the odor of soap, of cleaning.

He switched on the light and looked around. The floor was shining and clean under the light. He went into the kitchen and came back again.

"So you've been working," he said. "I didn't mean you to work; I told you to rest."

"I wanted to," she said, "I wanted to do it." She paused. "It wasn't so hard."

He looked down, frowning. "You shouldn't have worked like this."

He went to the kitchen to wash his hands. She came to the door following him. She looked at him and said, "It made me happy to do it."

He said nothing. "Didn't you want me to clean?" she said. "Don't you like it?"

"Yes," he said. "I like it."

7

AFTER supper, the man gathered up some dirty clothes, from a chair and from several nails, and said, "I'll take this to the laundry." He put them in a pillowcase; she thought of the pillowcase she had carried when she escaped from the hospital. It seemed already a long time ago, although it was only a little over a week. He went out and was gone a short time. When he came back, he said, "Maybe we can straighten up some." His chiffonier was cluttered with bottles, letters, a typical man's accumulation. He threw a good deal away and finally left only what he needed. "That looks better," he said. He moved some of the furniture, asking her advice on how it looked. The room became more orderly, more comfortable looking.

He took off his shoes and sprawled across the bed. As she had the night before, she sat in the armchair. She leaned back, and if it had not been for the light, might have closed her eyes and gone to sleep. Lassitude now poured into her, from the work she had done and from the summer's warmth. Her hair fell against her cheek, her head lying to one side, and she saw the man but indistinctly.

"Did you have any trouble shopping?" he said.

"No," she said. "I bought most of the things in an Italian store around the corner."

"That's a good place." He put his arms behind his neck.

"There are a lot of children in the street, aren't there?" she said. Strong arms. The cuffs of his shirt sleeves were pulled back, and she saw the heavy wrists and the hair of his forearm.

rt6rt

"This section swarms with children. Italians. They breed like flies, with poverty on one side and the church on the other."

Tiredness in her body. "Nobody seems to watch them."

"They live their own lives," he said.

She remembered her talk with Miss Child, who had lived in this city, maybe not so very far from here. But she could not have been one of these children, not as free, as hard. These children were living where nothing touched them.

"They remind me of my own childhood," the man said. "Although I lived in a different kind of place."

Her hair again fell before her eyes, darkening him. She said, "Where was it, where you were a child?"

"Oh, a small mining town in Ohio—Collins Bluff. A coal section."

"Tell me about it."

"It's hard to tell you about. The part I knew was where the miners lived. They lived in shacks, company shacks, I guess you've heard the expression. My father lived in one; it was pretty bad, always worrying about the rent, about paying back debts. And it was ugly. The streets unpaved usually pushing out into the country, into piles of slag. And yet—"

"Were there many children?"

"Oh yes. Miners have lots of children. But we were free for a while, although some kids went on the breakers at eight or nine and if they were big enough, were allowed into the mines at twelve, thirteen, to drive mules or some other job. I was free a little longer than most of them. My mother kept me in school, thought I'd get ahead. It's usually the mother who wants this."

"So what happened?"

"My mother died when I was sixteen and I ran away from home. I went into a mine."

Her hair like darkness, darkness taking him, covering him like the ground.

"How long?"

"Thirteen years."

She understood now his crouched shoulders.

"You left home?" she said.

"Yes, my father and I didn't get along. I only stayed before because of my mother. And when I left, one of my brothers, Jimmy, went along with me." He paused, seeming to think. "My father was a hard man. I remember—one day when I was just a kid, maybe four or five, I did something and he was going to beat me. I ran into the shack to my mother. He called to me to come out; he was going to beat me in a shed outside. I told my mother, 'Pop's going to lick me. Don't let Pop lick me.' I remember now the room where we were, just how it looked. For some reason, maybe the summer heat, the shutters were drawn. 'He won't lick you,' she said. Pop came in and I pressed behind her skirts. 'Where's John?' he said, angrily. 'He's here,' my mother said. 'I want him,' he said. 'Let him alone,' my mother said; 'you beat him too much.' My father came towards her as if he were going to get me, but he stopped and turned and went out of the room. I felt as if my mother had saved me from the most terrible beating of my life."

He sat up on the edge of the bed. "It's too bad to have to remember such things," he said. He went over to the window and stood looking down into the courtyard.

"My father lived about ten years, after I left home. I saw him several times before he died. We were both men then and liked each other."

8

Two boys walking alone a flat road, carrying blankets and bundles. Kentucky, Alabama, asking where? At the Trebebrecken Coal Corporation in Alabama, they got their first job, went down— The new sound of tunnels, hammers, explosions. They worked loading. It was continually damp; there were smells of gas, mule urine, hay. They were always tired; at night, sleeping in a crowded room, they tossed waiting for the shout, "Whistle," that seemed to come so soon.

"After a while Jimmy got sick and went home, but I stuck it out. Jimmy wrote me later he was in the mines in Ohio, to come back, but I didn't go. I liked Jimmy, but hated the place where I was born. I worked in various mines in the south and became a certified miner."

"What's that?" she said.

"It's— You have to know what an engineer knows, and maybe a little more. You have a group of men under you, and you supervise their work, working their places, timbering, drilling, loading— The main thing, according to the bosses, is to get out coal."

It was after that he saw his father again. The sense of death in his father. Pity. "A man whose woman has died ages quickly...

"My father thought it was good I was a certified miner. It paid eighteen dollars a week when I was working; that was pretty good. The men made ten, twelve dollars. Of course the work wasn't steady, maybe over a year what you really made was only nine, ten dollars a week. Still, it looked good." His face again, her hair, the darkness. "But then something happened."

"What?"

"I don't know. I began to get sick of it. For one thing I tried to get raises for the men under me. If I didn't work steady, they didn't work, and they were making a lot less than I was—they had families. Men with five, six children had no pay for two weeks, three weeks, a month. They got desperate, in the winter, and stole coal. This was how: there were a number of abandoned drifts—that is, tunnels straight into a hill, that they would go into to get coal. These drifts are dangerous—every once in a while one caved in and—"

"No!"

He paused. "Well, I got sick of it. I hated it. Suddenly I decided to leave the mines and I haven't been in a mine since."

Cities, west and east. "I'd been pretty handy with tools and when I was in Cleveland, I heard there was a call for men in machine shops. Not many shops will train men; they expect them to be experts and yet practically none of them give any training. It's only in Europe that men can learn by apprenticeship. I did the best I could, I went to libraries and got out books, I studied the way I had when I was in the mines. In the meantime I was getting some work. At first I bluffed; I learned, though, and kept picking things up. Lots of men in the shops are Germans; my family is German so a few of them were willing to help me. It wasn't easy, but it was better than the mines. I tried to get my brother, Jimmy, to do it, but he was married by that time and didn't want to change."

She asked him about his work. He told her he ran a metal lathe. "You've heard of lathes, they turn—" "Yes." Shafts, "threaded shafts for cranks" speed lathes, engine lathes, head lathes, drill presses, boring mills, gear cutters, turret lathes— She put her head in her hands. He described the lathes, the shop—the walls, belts, heat. She tried to see a lathe. Then "soap water," "head-stock," "cut." Men working, environment of skill, of measurement. She looked at his hands and seeing certain calluses and stains, made him explain what they were, and although she was unable fully to understand, the words he used were interesting to her.

"But the shop is like the mine," he said. "I don't know, it's the same thing everywhere." Tired of talking, he stood up. "I feel like a walk. Do you want to come?"

9

WITHOUT turning out the light, they went out. The courtyard, dark now, reminded her of the darkness the night he had brought her here. Two nights ago. She turned back to look at the house again. In several of the rooms of the building were lights; in one window a man sat in his undershirt, dark against the lighted room inside.

They went down the little passageway. When the gate had clanged shut behind them, she stood for a minute looking around her and the man stopped too. The street was shadowed, but in places there was a glow of store windows or street lamps. She looked up at the opposite building, up fire escapes blotted in metal shadow, rows of windows, the night pallor of brick and wood. Who lived in such a building? A child ran in the open doorway and she heard voices in the hall. In small groups, lit with the vague lights of the street, the children were still playing, but they were altered by the night—they were less strident and appeared to feel the weight of the dark. They walked slowly down the street, looking in store windows, at people. Italian faces, clean shaven but a few with handle-bar moustaches. As they came towards the corner, they heard the pulsing h'mp clop h'mp clop of a jazz band coming from the second story of a corner building. The windows of this floor were curtained, but over the curtains they could see electric bulbs covered with rose paper. "I think that's some Italian club holding a dance," he said. "Every Saturday night I've noticed it." They could occasionally see heads coming near the windows and the music pulsed into the street. There was a sound of voices and laughter.

They turned the corner and went past stores, most of them brightly lighted. One of the stores had the front curtained off with a high dark-green curtain, and as they passed, the door swung open and she saw men standing at a bar.

They turned a corner again and left the stores behind, going now along a street in the rear of their own, even quieter, having only rows of dark houses. Not as many children, not as many lights. They saw a man and woman leaning out of a window, talking to a man in the street. The man in the window said, "I can't get any relief with my son earning four dollars a week. So they've turned off my electricity and gas." Walked on. Quietness, a blind space between the uneven heights of the buildings. Some of the entrances were clean, with closed doors, others were dirty doorways open to any stranger. As they came towards the end of the street, they heard hurdy gurdy music; it was coming from a small merry-go-round mounted on an automobile. The merry-go-round was going rapidly around. All they could see at first was the wire enclosing it and a conical dome. As they approached, they saw that the narrow space inside was filled with excited children, each clinging to a little horse. The music pounded on, the children screamed with happiness; the music stopped, and the children got off, each one hopping down the small steps to the sidewalk. The manager of the merry-go-round was a dark businesslike foreigner who spoke to the children showing no interest, pushing them. Undismayed, they stood waiting to pay their fares again.

A little beyond the merry-go-round they turned the corner again, going back towards their own street. They were now on the street of the pushcarts, glowing still in the early evening although by certain signs, pieces of wilted lettuce on the sidewalk, fallen price cards, gaps at the curb, they could see that night would soon take the carts and the color away. Some distance further on, where the blur of electricity mounted the upper-story living quarters of the stores, was the church she had seen before, its wall on the same line with the street's building fronts. Its dull, yellow stone held up a golden cross into the night sky. "That's the church," the man said, "that produces so many children." They walked slowly on, the smells, the voices in the dark close and all their eyes saw, near them and alive. Now they had reached their street again and entered its quieter darkness. The children, still playing. Their steps loud in the passageway and the child sound ending. When they entered the courtyard, she saw that some of the lights in the house had gone out, but the house was not dead, not a blank of moon as it had been the first time she saw it. They entered, and left the night.

When they were in the room again, the man said, "Do you want to bathe tonight?"

"Yes, if I could."

"There's no tub in the building. I have some towels and you can heat yourself some water and bathe in the kitchen."

She went in the kitchen and put on the water and came back. They sat silent until the water boiled, a sound already familiar to her. He got her a towel and washcloth and, taking a nightgown, she went into the kitchen and closed the door. She put a newspaper on the floor and undressed. Naked, she rubbed the washcloth along her arms, her body; the warm water felt good on her flesh. When she was almost finished, the man called through the door, "Put some water on to heat for me." She put on the water for him, and rubbed herself completely dry; her body, though, still moist with the warmth and steam of the room. Her nightgown clung to her; she picked up her clothes. "Look out the window a minute," she called to the man. "All right," he said. She opened the door and ran to the bed.

The man turned around. "How did it go?" he said.

"All right. It felt good."

"Well, I'll have mine now."

She saw that he had laid out his bed on the floor. He went in the kitchen and closed the door and she heard him bathing. He splashed the water and once lost his footing and recovered it. After a while, he was quiet and she thought he must be drying himself.

"Okay?" he called.

"Yes."

He came in wearing his pyjamas. "Well—" he said, yawning, "if you're ready." He put out the light. Moving cautiously across the room, he got into his bed on the floor.

"Good night," he said.

"Good night."

She was tired; almost as her eyes closed, she fell asleep. A few minutes or a few hours later, she sprang awake. There had been a loud crash in the hallway. The man was sitting up on the floor. "You're not frightened," he said. "That's Rocco, the Italian who lives upstairs. When he gets depressed and needs to relieve his feelings, he throws a meatbone downstairs for his dog to chase." She heard the pattering of the dog's footsteps as he carried the bone back upstairs. "It doesn't matter what time of night or day it is, when he gets that way, he throws the meatbone."

She looked around the dark room and outside at the night.

"Well, we'll try to get to sleep again," he said.

She closed her eyes and immediately was asleep.

10

SUNDAY. She woke into warmth, the sun was on the bed. She was lying on her stomach and as she raised up, along her body she felt stiffness from the work she had done the day before. She turned; the man was still sleeping, in shadow. The floor—his body was solid, stretched out, his breath slowly rising and falling; he looked strong and she thought of the many kinds of work he had done. Sunday morning. She listened, propped on her elbows, to its silence. It was quiet everywhere, the city was as quiet as it would get. She thought of the Sunday morning before, in the rooming house, when she had woken with the woman sleeping beside her. Life, death. Not only her own death but the death of the years in the hospital. She pressed her face into her hands, Forget, take away death. She pushed back her hair and looked downward at the man. He was motionless, his eyes closed, breathing evenly. Eyelids. Once in the hospital she had been awakened at night and feeling restless had gone into Miss Cummings' room. Miss Cummings was lying still; all at once she had thought that she was dead. Her eyelids in particular had the blank look, the fixity of death. As she looked now at the man, the likeness to death returned. Yet not the same. He was moving; as she watched, he opened his eyes.

"Hello," he said, turning towards her.

"Hello," she said.

"Sleep well?"

"Yes."

They had looked at each other; they looked away. The sunlight almost reached the back of the room—in a jagged line it leaped up furniture, walls. The floor, the boards from which the original paint had almost worn away, was bleached, scrubbed looking. The whole room was clean. She thought he, too, was noticing the cleanness, and avoided his eyes.

"How do you feel?" he said.

"Fine."

They dressed, she in the front room and he in the kitchen. The room was warm; she dropped off her nightgown and as she bent for her brassiere, the sun hit across her, like a blade on her belly. A horse stamped; she looked outward at the light.

They ate breakfast together. Afterward the man said, "Do you want to come with me and get the morning paper?" She nodded and they went out. The sky over them; buildings; the wash of hot blue. In the street, she saw that the children had yielded to Sunday and in their cleaner clothes, stood quietly, making only a few awkward movements towards freedom. A boy was dipping a patent-leather sandal in a puddle of water that had oozed out from under the closed front of a laundry. Little girls held clean handkerchiefs in their hands, laughed, and when the impulse overcame them, ran in their stiff dresses. The street was changed.

They bought a paper at a corner newsstand and went back to the room. The sun was in it, silent as it had been earlier in the morning. Its pressure was memory and pain; in the hospital she had had the Sunday paper too, she had wanted it; it took her back to the time before her brother's death when they had read it together. Its smell in particular strengthened her recollection and she had half believed she was alive— Brother, brother, if we were not dead— When she had read the paper, in the room at the hospital, she would go to the window and look out towards the remote horizon of life.

The man sat in the armchair near the bed; she was on the bed. FRANCE VOTES ARMAMENTS NEW RAY TO STOP AIRPLANE MOTORS "In event of war—"

"It talks here about war. Do you think there will be war?" she said.

"Yes, I guess so," he said.

"Why?"

"I don't know."

"But why, what will they fight about?"

"I don't know. Nobody knows except maybe those who won't die."

She went on reading. "Ivan Michailoff, Macedonian revolutionary leader, is reported killed at—" "Reliable military sources said late today that—" "Labor leaders declared yesterday they would not submit to government's 'work or starve' edict." "Springfield, Ill. Three men were injured, two seriously, when an Illinois Central freight train was dynamited three miles south of here early today. The blast derailed the locomotive and nine of the 120 empty cars of the train. Investigation officials said they believed a coal miners' dispute was behind the dynamiting—" She read this item aloud to him. "Why do miners dynamite the trains?" she said.

"The line carried scab coal, probably."

"What's that?"

"Coal mined by strikebreakers."

His eyes were dark, darkness out of the past. Out of his past, out of her past? The darkness grew; she trembled. The man was bent over a section of the paper; she looked at him, at his crouched shoulders. She no longer read but kept looking at him, at his head, at his hands holding the paper. The sun behind him touched him in a faint outline; the outline reminded her of something. She lay watching; he dropped a section of the paper and put his head back on the chair as though trying to rest.

She said, "Why don't you lie down here on the bed?"

He came to the bed; he lay towards the head and she towards the foot. Now that he was close to her, she was afraid and wanted to get up. Perfectly still, she began to notice a quickening of her blood. Breath—breathing shallowly, the breath hardly entering her, hardly caught before it was breathed out again. She no longer wanted to get up; she was confused by the deepening silence of her body.

She looked into his eyes. The room was changed, he bent over her and his hand touched her side. "No!" she said. And yet gradually she was pressed back, she knew that it was happening and the pain she felt became nothing to the life. At that moment she forgot death; it was only later, when they lay quietly resting, that she remembered.

11

AT NIGHTFALL they went to bed together. In the morning she was still in bed when he left. He kissed her; she heard his steps go down the stairs and across the courtyard. As they faded, she closed her eyes and lay without thought, her veins drumming with sleep. An hour went by and she heard the sound of the city, that she had never stopped hearing since she came up into it from the tunnel under the river. Size, measureless size around her, breath rising from millions of men, from all their motions, desires. An automobile, a block or two away as she could tell by the sound, crossed a manhole cover, giving it a metallic clang. The sound entered her: fear in the rooming house, the keys, cries screaming "I want I want—" words voices whisper.

She had accepted life.

She got up and slowly dressed. As she made the awkward mechanical movements of dressing, she thought of what had happened. She thought, I have taken him, his life into my own. Yet not life, she was born out of death and soon to return again to death. He must know it, tonight he must know it.

She went into the kitchen and ate, but hardly feeling hunger. His life in her had touched her death; it could not quicken it. A spasm of darkness, of faintness passed over her. If with life— No. She went back into the other room and began to make the bed. The imprint of his body was still beside her own; she looked at it and touched it. She saw a small blood stain; the faintness increased, she lowered her head.

A little before five, she noticed the sound of horses being driven into the stable. Horses and men coming to eat, to sleep. Not long after it, she heard the first clang of the gate. The men of the building were coming, soon he would come. The inscription in the book, "To my son John." She went to the kitchen and began to cook dinner. As she was busy, or as some grease was hissing, she failed to hear him, either at the door or crossing the outer room. She looked up and saw him in the kitchen door, hungry and tired-looking.

"John," she said, going to him.

He took her in his arms and kissed her.

They ate as they had eaten before but she felt a certain restraint in him. The light burned on the white table top, gradually the light of the outer room faded in the door and she knew the other room was getting dark. Darkness, the coming of night. Night and sleep, and beyond sleep, death. Suddenly he said, "Harriet, I love you."

"I love you," she said.

"I want you to marry me."

Now she must tell him. "I can't," she said.

"Why not? Why can't you?"

"Because I'm insane."

She saw the exploding darkness in his eyes, the terror. If there had been pity, she could not have looked at him again. But in terror she found strength.

"Don't be afraid," she said. "I died. I'm not really alive. And yet I wanted to have life." She told him the story of her brother's death, of her years in the hospital. "It's called 'cyclic insanity.' Part of the time it's like a terrible dream, the 'manic' period. I'm not violent, just terribly afraid and lost. Then following that is a 'depressive' state. I'm in what's called a 'recovered' period now."

"Isn't a permanent cure possible?"

She hesitated. "Yes, but I can't believe it's possible. I can't."

"I can."

She turned away from him, almost in anger. Dr. Revlin. "You can still have hope."

"I don't believe it's possible, for me."

"Why not?"

She had not even meant to tell him about Dr. Revlin. "Because a doctor, one of the best in the country, Dr. Georges Revlin, tried to cure me and failed."

"Did he give up?"

"No."

"Then how can you say he failed?"

"He did." She described the final attempt he had made. Under his questioning, she had to admit to him that Dr. Revlin had said there was still hope. She also told him that he had apparently been willing for her to escape.

"Maybe he knew more than you think."

"No—"

He sat silent for a minute. "What is it—" he said, "don't you want to be cured?"

She said nothing.

"I think I understand," he said. He took her hand and gripped it. "You were brave to tell me what you did. It doesn't change things. I still love you. That's all that matters."

"But it's wrong. Can't you see it's wrong?"

"No," he said, "I can't."

12

THAT EVENING they talked together for a long time, lying on the bed. She felt, in speaking, the same lack of separateness she had felt the day before; she felt that he could understand her as she understood herself. His strength, his kind eyes; the sense of his nearness that she wanted and that went beyond reason. His room was part of him; around him it gave her courage. She had much to say to him; if it were not for his strength and their lack of separateness, she could not have told him. She thought of how she had spoken to Dr. Revlin. This was different. Dr. Revlin had been a conscience, but she was speaking now to the part of herself that was not conscience, the part that suffered; what she told John now was herself as she was to herself. In an accident which she described to him, her brother had been killed; she had seen his life crushed out with intolerable violence, death had taken his place in her. She said, "We both died." She went on and told him about her childhood; her words were vague sometimes, but she came back to what seemed important; he had a part in this re-turn, to what was important. When they had come again to the time of her brother's death, he said, "Your parents must have suf-fered." She was going to say something, but uncertainty—like the uncertainty of a person who has two things upon his tongue—kept her from it. He noticed her silence and respected it; when she went on speaking, she began to feel peace, such as she had not known in a long time, in his presence, in the understanding that in spite of the difficulty, the confusions of what she had to say, remained unbroken between them. She felt as she had when he brought her to his room the first night and she had seen his bed. Looking at him, she said, "I can't understand why it has been so easy to tell you this." He asked her about the hospital; she spoke of what it meant to be in it, to be insane. "Manic depressive," the horror of darkness and the drop into the state of fear and dream that was not dream; which continued, had intervals of unconsoling sleep, and carried its suffering into memory. "I used to sometimes fear even more the return to memory, to knowing I was dead." She described baths, restraint, forced feedings, she let him see in its full extent the agony of her years in the hospital. His eyes and his voice closed around her suffering. She told him of rooms and corridors where the depressives were, of the unhuman silence, slow breaths that could just be heard; and she told him too of the looks of recognition, when they first came, that were a terrible resurrection. "Many of them are old women—how many times had they died?" The wing with the incurables, in which she had lived with Dr. Revlin's permission; as she was speaking out of that part of her which could not recognize Dr. Revlin, she told him only what it had meant to her, a place of refuge from eyes that could see in her always her own and her brother's death. She told him about Miss Cummings, about other women on the floor—not, though, about Miss Barrett. He asked what her room was like and she described it: bed, wardrobe, window—"Everything has a lock, even the hot air ventilator. The nurses have rings of keys" unlock and lock "You're always hearing it, the sound of the lock—" "What were the nurses like?" he said. "Middle aged, used to the work. They're all right, only— But they can't help being in their own world—and living away from us. There was one nurse, though—" She told him about Miss Child, who had been a friend, and told him of the night of her escape. "Do you think," he said, "Miss Child could have helped you, could have left the door open?" "I've thought of it," she said. "But how could she know? How could she know I would try the door?" Suddenly something came into her mind that was separate from anything she had said, that came from the other part of her. "Maybe," she said, "she forgot because she was thinking of what I had said; I had practically said I wanted to escape. Sometimes people do things unconsciously, Dr. Revlin said, because it's what they want to do." "That's true," he said. She tried to forget; the room grew darker; they rested their heads on their arms, looking at each other.

"Could I ask you something?" she said. "It's foolish of me, I guess—"

"What?"

"Do you think I'll have a baby?"

He smiled. "You might, but it doesn't happen so easily, usually. We'll have to be more careful, though."

"How do you mean?"

He explained. "Oh," she said, "I didn't know that." Repulsion, again the world as something unknown; the man singing in the evening behind the rooming house: threat. Accept, take it as it is. And looking again at John, at his face and particularly his shadowed eyes, she regained suddenly the knowledge of his understanding, of his identity with herself and of herself with him.

13

SHE FOUND, in the days immediately following, that she could depend fully on the understanding between herself and John. Its strength continued under the adjustments and the matter-of-fact details of their life; she was always aware of it underneath and knew that it was something that would endure and that she could hold to. It was a peculiar awareness between them, as though part of herself were in him and part of him were in her, so that certain things could be taken for granted. Yet the very strength of their understanding caused her occasional misgivings: unwillingly she looked ahead and saw those final issues they had denied and which would eventually have to be faced. What would the end be? What would it be for him? He loved her and had taken her on her own terms; yet could he know? After a while she deliberately made herself forget, giving herself up to what she knew could not be changed.

Daily problems, that she enjoyed discussing with him, helped to keep her mind from the other things. An immediate practical problem was that of washing her clothes, and possibly his. One evening she said, "John, I want to do the wash. I don't like you to be sending out the wash; it costs you too much." He tried to argue with her, but she said, "I want to try it," and looking out the window, she said, "Do you think we could put up a line here anywhere?" "No, I'm afraid there's no way to put one up from the windows. But maybe there's a place on the roof." "Why, can we get up on the roof!" she said. "Yes, there's a way up." "Let's see!"

She made him take her at once. As they started up, she realized she had not been to the top of the house before. The stairs now were dark; she felt them swaying with their weight as they climbed upward. She could not overcome her usual nervousness on the stairs, and held to John's arm. Suddenly a stair tread gave way under her; John caught her and said, "That's pretty bad, isn't it." From the shock, she began to laugh. When they reached the floor landing above, Rocco's dog began furiously barking through the door; a voice in Italian quieted him. This was fortunately the top; it was dark—there was only a gas jet burning, no skylight as there had been at Mrs. Helios'. They found a door and a narrow stairway to the roof.

The sun, she saw when they opened the door on the roof, had not yet set. The air was warm, the day's heat only slowly leaving it—the flat tar paper of the roof was still sticky from the heat. In the center of the roof were two chimneys covered with yellow tiles; fastened to a parapet that went around the edge of the roof were some posts.

"Could those posts be used for a line?" she said.

"I guess you could use them for that."

"Yes, they'd be fine." She could see the line of clothes already; she could see just where to put it. "Come here," she said. They walked to the edge of the parapet and looked over. To the rear was the yard of another house on the street behind them which had been made into a garden. "I never knew that was there," he said. The garden, with small benches and walks, was separated from the rear yards on either side by a high wall. They walked all around the parapet, looking at neighboring yards and rooftops. Many roofs had water tanks, she noticed; on one roof they saw a line of wash. They stood together, with the heat lessening around them, silent, looking across the roofs at the setting sun, its circle cut by chimneys. Here was a different city, the spaces never seen from the streets; she was glad they had come up, and that she knew it was there around them as they went down into the dark house.

When they were safely back in the room again, she discussed

certain other problems of the wash with him—how she would iron, whether he needed starch in his shirts, what to wash the clothes in. He had an answer for every question—"Buy a small electric iron." "Never starch my shirts; I don't like them starched." "Buy a galvanized iron tub—" "Now when you have the tub," he went on; he explained the art of syphoning. She listened; she suddenly realized he was as much interested in the wash as she was.

She found the actual work of washing not as easy as it had sounded; certain practical difficulties developed. She had trouble in heating the water. Ironing was particularly hard. Slowly, however, she learned, and in time was able to do an ordinary wash creditably. When, for the first time, she gave John a shirt to put on that she had entirely washed and ironed herself, he said, "That's the first shirt a woman has washed for me since my mother died."

"Is it all right?" she said.

He rubbed his hands over it.

"It's all right," he said.

14

Darkness was slowly falling and they were eating in the kitchen; beyond the strength of the electric light she could see the light of the other room fading. Food. She thought, as she ate, of the dining hall at the hospital, of its bare walls, its tables, the peculiar rattle of chinaware. She was thankful for this quiet, this peace.

"I've been thinking of that tread in the stairs," John said. "Rocco ought to speak to Mr. Varchi about it."

"Mr. Varchi?"

"He's the owner of the building."

Owner. The word was peculiarly surprising: somebody owning this building, this room.

"Mr. Varchi, is that Italian?" she said.

"Yes. He's a real estate agent and he's done very well during the depression. He's bought several buildings around here by taking over the mortgages."

"What does that mean, 'taking over the mortgages'?" she said. He explained the meaning of a mortgage, and how mortgages are foreclosed. "The value of real estate now is so low that there's no equity above the mortgage in lots of cases, sometimes not even enough to cover it."

"'Equity?'" she said. He explained this term and when she finally understood, she said, "And all the buildings you see are like that?"

"Almost all." Getting up, he said, "I'm going up and ask Rocco if he'll complain about that step. It's on his flight and he's the one that ought to complain about it."

While he was gone, she started the dishes. The thought of Mr. Varchi disturbed her, of somebody owning this building. It had seemed simply a refuge, something quiet, sure, existing in itself. Now with this new thought about it, it changed. "Owner." Nobody owned the hospital. Ownership was something of the outside world, like money. Threat, always the unsuspected threat.

John came back and said, "Well, it's no good. Rocco's afraid to say anything. He's probably behind in his rent." After a moment he said, "I'm going around and tell Mr. Varchi myself. He has an office near here. Want to come?"

"All right."

They went out together and after a five minute walk, turned into a block under the El. In the middle of the block, John pointed to a window on which a sign said: UNITED REALITIES. "That's his office," he said. The office was large, above the street level; a few photographs of "available properties" stood in the window, in back of which a green curtain hung. To go inside, they had to go up a small flight of steps and through a narrow door. The office was high-ceilinged, bare; there were two desks, a safe, and not much other furniture. Several men, Italians, were sitting on cane chairs; one of them, short, fat, with folds of flesh under his eyes, turned to them and said, "Good evening—ah, Mr. Kohler."

"Good evening," John said. "Mr. Varchi, I want to introduce you to my wife."

"Please to know you, Mrs. Kohler," Mr. Varchi said, getting up. She shook his hand.

"I came to ask about something," John went on. "My wife will have to go up to the roof occasionally to hang up the wash—"

"Yes, that's a quite all right," Mr. Varchi said.

"But when my wife went up the stairs a few days ago, one of the steps gave way. It's broken—"

"Where a you mean?"

"One of the steps just before you come to Mr. Rocco's floor."

"Yes?"

"We'd like to have it fixed."

"Uh," Mr. Varchi said; she could see his eyes change. "I see about it."

"If it isn't fixed, you know you're liable to get yourself in for a damage suit."

"Well, I fix. Of course—broken step."

All Mr. Varchi's friends stared at them with eyes like his; it frightened her. John said good-by and she was glad they were leaving. When they were outside, she said, "He didn't like what you said, about the damage suit."

"Well, he'll fix it," John said.

They walked back along the street and she looked up at the El structure. As they came to the corner, a train roared past, its wheels grating and the coaches blurred above them. She said, "Is this the Sixth Avenue El?"

"Yes."

"Would you like to see the place where I had my room, the rooming house?"

"Sure I would."

It was uptown; they took a train at the nearest station and after a short ride, got off at Eighteenth Street. As they walked back along Sixth Avenue to the street where she had lived, she felt a peculiar excitement. What would it be like? It seemed a long time since she had lived here. They turned the corner into the street; it looked just the same as it had. The same houses. The men who seemed always to be in the doors, in collarless shirts, leaning, waiting for possible roomers, were still there. The street-level doors, always open, revealed the dark corridors she remembered; in their depths lights were now appearing, for darkness was beginning to fall. They walked up the street and towards the Seventh Avenue end of the block, she stopped and said, "That's it, across there."

A flight of steps; the door she knew. As she looked, from the stone front all the known interior began to throb in her, alive— the hallway with its gas bracket, the furniture at the foot of the staircase, the stairs up to the orange-painted top floor, and like a dull blaze, the skylight overhead. Long week, room, closed door and the sound of rain "reminds me of the tropics" the sun. Mrs. Helios. She thought, I wish I could see George. If I could just see him. As she watched, as though she had made it happen, the door slowly opened and George came out. He stood still, in his dirty white suit, his convict hair straight up from his forehead; he took a breath of air and with a casual glance at the street, went back in.

"Did you see George!" she said.

"Who, him—"

"Yes!" She had told him about George. She said, "I'm glad I saw him."

When they had finished looking at the building and the street, they walked slowly back to the El, and took a train downtown again.

Freedom— The visit to the scene of her first week, of her first freedom, brought back in a wave the memory of her meeting with John, and what it had meant. Except for it the future would have been death. There had been nothing ahead; he had given her everything. Rest, food, refuge. He had given her more than that; that had been much but he had given her much more. Understanding. And more, his love. Love that made his giving no longer giving, that made her able to give in return. She could give; she could return something to him. And yet—how could the dead give anything to the living?

They were walking back from the downtown El station. Interrupting her thoughts, a sudden sound made her and John stop. They were on a street whose house fronts and first floor windows were close to the sidewalk. From a window close beside them, a sudden guitar note sounded; a moment later they heard a group of men begin singing:

> "Csak egy kis lány van a világon
> Az is az én drága galambom
> A jó Isten de szerethet engem
> Hogy Tégedet adott énnékem."

The song, with the throb of the trembling guitar, deepened. A curtain blew in and they could see a group of men sitting at a table. When they finished the song, John, who was only a few feet from them, said, "*Aggy Isten.*"

"*Aggy Isten,*" one of the men answered. "*Magyar maga is?*"

"No. I just know some Hungarian. I used to work with Hungarians."

"Where you work!"

"In mines, different places."

"You hear!" the man said, turning around. "A miner! Where, what mine?"

"The Trebebrecken Pit in Alabama, the Troublas Point Pit in Kentucky—"

"You know anywhere a miner, tall, has a mark like this on his cheek, his name Carl Coury?"

"No. No, I don't."

"My wife's brother." The men had gotten up and were crowding to the window. "You come in?"

"No, we're just on our way home. We liked your song."

"We sing for you again, no?"

"Yes, sure."

They sang the same song again, the guitar accompanying it with a steady thrumming sound:

"*A jó Isten de szerethet engem*
Hogy Tégedet adott énnékem."

When they had finished, John said, "Thank you. It was beautiful." He hesitated and said, "What does your song mean?"

"It means—" One of the men stopped to think. "It means, 'There is only one girl—that is my love. The dear God must love me, he gave you to me.'"

John laughed. "It's a true song," he said.

He thanked them again and they said good-by; they walked on, through the streets which were now dark. The night had fallen and it was silent except for the sound of some children, still playing in the shadows of the houses.

15

EACH DAY dawned now with sun against the shades or the shadow of rain. She got up early and made breakfast for him: this small interval of time with him before he went to work, although they were for the most part silent and busy, meant much to her; it was an understanding of habit, a new understanding that now took its place beside the closeness of their first love. The fitting of lives together—yet when she thought it, "life," there was always the doubt. She turned away from it—she thought only now of each day ahead of her. During the working hours they would be separated, he at the shop, she through the day alone. Yet the day of waiting was good; it had its meaning.

She had begun to teach herself to cook. About the midday meal she cared nothing, but she began to prepare cooked meals for dinner. At the beginning he had often taken her out to eat—with his hard physical work he needed substantial food. As she learned to cook, he stopped going out and she looked forward each day to preparing a good meal for him, and making it appetizing. She was helped by the proprietress of the Italian grocery shop she went to, a woman who was a skilled cook. "A stew? Hah. That's easy." And she described exactly the method of cooking, Piacenza vista in her words, odorous morality. "That he will like, the man, hah?"

Washing, cooking—tasks to do until the hour when he would return. These days were never long, but went by in hours of steady work, or if without work, in the sense of life. All that she did had meaning, was placed against the terrible vacancy of her years in the hospital. Peace. Sun over the roof, the parapet, the courtyard, the passageway. Warmth, gradual healing. Around her, time's progress in the city's sound, slow, warm, tender.

In the late afternoon she began to quicken with the sense of his coming. Now he would be going through the last hour, the last half-hour of his work—the lathe, the metal fading in the afternoon light. Working, knowing his work. Like the women in the factory—she saw his arms. At last, the machine stilled; now he would be changing from his oil-stained overalls, he would be going out into the streets.

When he came home, the evening became different. As if some power burned and sprang from him shattering the stillness of the day, and in his stepping through the door her body was given a new shape. Now there would be the evening's hours ahead, to deepen into the further hours of night. Evening; most surely their own. In this space of time, complete, she lived in the hearing and loudness of the present, and what had been or was to be did not touch her.

There was once, though, that the past returned; it was partly through him. Lying together on the bed early one evening, they heard a radio being played in some adjacent building. It was an indistinct sound, but when somebody turned the control dial, a sudden burst of music poured out. John said unexpectedly, "Would you like a radio?" "No," she said. "Why?" Before her, as clear as though she were looking at it, was a room in which she sat with some twenty other women. Each of them sat on a separate chair; each was quiet, not talking, hardly moving. Most of them wore poorly laundered clothes, their hair was poorly knotted, uncared for. The room was like a cheap hotel lobby—with its varnished floor and potted palms. Against one wall stood a cabinet radio; in front of it two women sat who were just beginning to "recover." They had at times enough interest to speak a sentence or two to each other; one of them occasionally moved the dials of the radio. Although she sat in complete passiveness herself, she noticed a sound of steps and a nurse came in, bringing a visitor.

Visitor and nurse stopped; the two women at the radio looked up. Immediately one of the women turned and buried her head in her arms.

"Why?" John said. "Nothing," she said. "Dear, hold me, hold me just a minute."

16

THE FOLLOWING morning, she finished her work early and went out for a walk by herself, to wash from her in the streets the mood that still remained from the night before. The swaying stairs, with their stale plaster and wood-rot odor; she thought of the stairs at the hospital, strong, washed, angular. Once, going downstairs from a third floor depressive ward, she had looked through the railings at a turn where she could see a half flight further down. In the middle of a step stood a woman, a patient, holding a mop; on the landing below her was a pail of black water. The woman was evidently thinking, she was making a great effort to think, but when she noticed that somebody was coming, her eyes immediately became vacant. This woman merged with the woman of the night before and other faces came back. A stout woman sitting in a wicker chair in an outside corridor of a depressive ward, a girl who silently wove mats in the Occupational Therapy room, a girl who explained the "theory of numbers." The faces felt like a film that only finally disappeared in the life of the street. Life, the children, men and women. She walked slowly, looking at every face around her for the hardness of life.

She came to the pushcarts. Shadowed by white cloth or canvas spread above them, in some cases making a complete canopy over the sidewalk, were the fresh piles of lettuce, scallions, dandelions, celery, turnips, all wet and glistening, watered apparently from little watering cans that stood near them. Further down she saw the front of the church, always cold and dull in spite of the sun; beyond it, the El which blocked the street. On the El a train roared, long, sectioned, massive with sound. She kept walking until she was under the shadows of the El steelwork, in the permanent half dark and the sound of the train. She turned and walked along this darker street, in which only narrowed sun slanted down to the sidewalks; she passed bars behind blank windows, alcohol wetting the air with sweetness. Stores, many empty. The street as she walked along it grew in heat and darkness, unstirred air holding the sun like metal. She felt oppressed and yet wanted oppression, the oppressive weight of the street. No past, no future, no thought, only the street.

In the middle of a long block, on a board alongside of a building entrance she saw a sign in large letters: GIRL WANTED, SECOND FLOOR. She stopped, at once remembering how she had looked for work, when NO HELP WANTED or closed doors had taken the place of this welcoming sign written in black crayon. Work, the women she had seen in the factory windows. To have worked, to have had a job then would have meant, what—? "Life." Death, stirring in her the images of the night before, of that morning. She had said, "I still want to look for work." Escape from memory, death backward. Here was work offered, "girl wanted." Try? What she could make would help John, she knew he was not earning much and he occasionally sent money to his brother, Jimmy. Jimmy had three children. There would be less time for housework; it would be hard, perhaps, but that did not matter. Black script of the sign, it was written in a large crude handwriting, GIRL WANTED, SECOND FLOOR; it pressed on her eyes. When she looked away, its image floated in the air. It was everywhere, repeating itself, urging her, Try. She slowly entered the building. A wide dirty wooden staircase on which a large section of painters' canvas, splotched with white paint, had been stretched. At the second floor landing was a single closed door; through the door she heard a murmur of machines and voices. I. FARBMAN. She pushed the door open.

A long room spread out before her. At one end, crowded together, were ten sewing machines at which girls and women were working. Taking up a good part of the room was a long table at which more women and girls and one or two men were sitting sewing, their arms moving steadily, identically. In front of each one, fastened in the table, was a tall spindle of thread like a sign of inexhaustible labor. They were evidently making dresses; the table was littered with pieces of dress goods that moved, jerked with their work. To the right of the table were several racks of dresses and near them two ironing boards; at these a man and woman stood and took the dresses quickly as they were finished, ironed them, and hung them on the racks. The dresses were beautiful, delicate; they hung in many tints behind the plain dresses the working girls wore. Near her a tall man stood at a table by himself with a number of bolts of cloth, one of which he was cutting. There was other work going on in the room, every inch of floor was used. A tide of work, of sound met her. Fatigue. Needles pulled, thrust like a tic. The faces changed and in her mind bent over the frames, the mats, of the Occupational Therapy room. Therapy? This wave of work; this was life. She backed against the door. "Have those seams pinked," a middle-aged man said and turning to her, said, "Hello?"

She tried to speak. "I saw your sign downstairs," she said, "that you needed a girl."

"Yeah—well, you the girl?"

"I need work."

"We need somebody should start right now."

"All right, I can start now."

"You ever examine dresses?"

"No."

As if he had little time, he took her over to a rack of dresses, pulled out a dress, and said, "When you sew a seam on the machine, when you come to the end, it leaves a piece of thread. Here's one, see? I want you should find these and cut them off— nice and close, and not cut the dress. See?"

She put her fingers in the handle holes of the scissors he gave her and cut a thread.

"Not like that," he said. "Gimme the scissors."

He took the scissors and held them not by the handles, but by the blades. Rapidly he cut off a thread. "It's faster you hold them this way," he said. "Not so much chance you cut the dress. Try it."

She took the scissors the way he said and began to snip, began cutting the threads, hunting for them awkwardly. How many— in the hems, belt, sides, under the arms, in the neck? The man watched her; she finished the dress and did several more, working as fast as she could. He left her, came back. "About the pay— three fifty a week." He saw her hesitate and said, "Times are hard, understand? I try to be fair. Make it four dollars."

She nodded. She remembered the many places at which she had been turned away, in spite of offering to work "for anything." These other girls, women, did they get more? How did they live?

"Your hours are from seven to twelve, and twelve-thirty to five."

"All right."

He hesitated. "What's your name?"

"Harriet Kohler." "Kohler?" She spelled it for him. "All of these dresses are ready," he said, pointing to the dresses on the rack. She began quickly working, cutting as fast as she could. Numberless threads. When she had been at work only a little while, she became an unnoticed part of the shop; she was a part of its work. In an hour she had done eight dresses, was working more skillfully; she knew the seams, where to cut. She felt the pace of the hurrying arms around her; her arms, her fingers quickened. She began to feel the heat. Threads of heat, of sweat. Every forehead, she noticed, was sweaty; her own forehead was wet. At the front end of the shop, iron shutters were pushed open but no air came in; the ceiling was low and the heat of the irons, of the bodies at work, settled motionless and oppressive. She felt sweat trickle down her back—she worked on, faster, automatic, fastening to her heart the thud of irons, the sound of spindles unwinding, of needles puncturing cloth. The work no longer re- minded her of the hospital; it was competitive, bitter. She soon could remember, see, or think of nothing past the threads she cut, that fell in an endless rain.

17

THE FOLLOWING morning she came to the shop at five minutes to seven. Mr. Farbman nodded to her; she went to the dress rack and picked up the scissors. She was beginning where she had left off; the time between was lost. John, "I don't like you to take this job." His voice, lost, gone, annihilated in the scissors now moving, she cut threads with a movement that hardly opened the scissors. The threads, straight or twisted, fell and raveled softly in the floor at her feet. The work of the room was beginning, she could feel it with the heat, the irons heating, the bodies making their own heat, sweat forming. A full day, today would be longer; she must save a little strength to reach evening. John had accepted her decision. Now she would know like him the tiredness of the day's work, the peace of fatigue. She already knew the difference her work would make, the fact that she too was working. Only these first days would be hard—then she would become used to it, like him. Acceptance, the knowledge of work. As she cut, she looked at the faces around her. Different, marked differently by labor, few unmarked. There was a Negro girl who fitted dresses on a dummy, working skillfully. With her it was the eyes which, like dark holes, did not change their expression. The work became a sound in her ears; iron, spindle, scrape, cut, hiss. Faces. Mr. Farbman came over and said, "You've got enough of those dresses done. Let them go for a while, I want you should do something else." He brought her to a small peculiarly-shaped machine which she had not noticed before. "I want you should learn to pink." To pink meant to run seams through a machine which cut a fancy saw-toothed edge on them. Seam by seam, she was always working with seams. Machine, scissors. The Negro girl had pins in her mouth, she took material from the man with the bolts of cloth, the cutter. Must save her strength, the sun moved its strips along the floor. She could feel the heat like a cloud roll down the roofs, fill the streets, enter the room. Scalded air in front of the shutters trembled; the irons sent up rays and ripples of heat. The clock moved, the dresses knew no sweat, set their loveliness against their bodies. Hospital, forget—she cut with the scissors, cut thread, cut memory until the present burned alone in the threads falling.

As the week went on, she learned more about the shop. The cutter, or "designer," had no fear of the boss; she heard Mr. Farbman say to him, one morning, "Joe, you make more than I do." She learned from the talk in the shop that Mr. Farbman had come from Germany. She also learned that when she was almost too exhausted to stand, she could get a short rest by going to the lavatory. She spoke there once to the colored girl; she came from Florida where she had nine brothers and sisters. "Two of them are comin' up to live with me, they're starvin'." The days flowed through her arms and left her weak until, when she saw John in the evenings, new strength returned. What she thought of now was Saturday, the end of the week, the end of work, when she could really rest.

On Saturday morning, as she began work, it seemed that because it was the last day of the week, it was the hardest. Night now would never come; work had grown to take in all time, she no sooner left the shop than she was coming to it again, the time between lost itself, was swallowed in sleep. Only sweat existed, the sound of sewing machines, irons, the El. The repeated roaring of the El galvanized her through moments of pain, tiredness became a doorless room. Pay. As hour by hour passed, she thought of her pay at five o'clock. Money, the meaning of her work. Freedom. From where she stood, she could see a small clock on the wall. Five minutes, how many threads, how many cuts of the scissors. To save herself, she had learned how to ease her arms by taking slightly more time on the lower part of a dress. Noon; she rested rather than ate. Afternoon began, coursed in the snip of scissors, the shadows of cloth casting their bruises on her arms. To some distant shoulder, breast, they would pass, changed, the stains of love. Love. Memory. Time crossed the minutes slowly; at four o'clock she felt that the hour ahead was as long as the day behind her. Then, with need, thought died and after so many hundred and hundred threads, so many known, foreknown motions of shoulders, arms, fingers, the shop became quiet. Five o'clock. Mr. Farbman came over to her and unbelievably handed her her money. "Be here at seven Monday." She held the money, which was in an envelope, in her hand; she could feel coins—it would not be a full four dollars because she had not worked a full week. The meaning of the money broke through her exhaustion. Money, making her one with millions, joining her in a new way to life. Life. And tomorrow she could rest. Holding the money, she walked out of the shop into the street crowded with others, like her, going home from work. She was no longer tired and coming to the house, went in and without knowing how it had happened, she found herself lying on the bed in the room, her eyes open and in her hand, gripped tightly, the pay envelope. John, come soon. Must not close her eyes, closed her eyes and the thread of sound ran thin. Peace fell.

He touched her and she sat up. What?—still in her hand. She handed him the pay envelope.

18

"HEY, COME here!" close "*Gli odo giá dirmi—*" Rising light, the street at dawn. Men in working clothes passed her, children carrying loaves of bread. "*—son stanchi.*" "*Anch'io lo so.*" Heard, half heard the sound of these voices—"*La morte.*"

It was Monday and all the day before was gone. She walked by houses, by stores and entranceways, thinking, Now it is gone. "*—omai gl'Itali*" yet it was not gone, it was still here, she could feel it more real than the street—the El upward, the houses— through them it was still here. "*—giorni.*" She felt his lips and felt his hand on her breast, the hand that did not change it. Silence, the form of time—extended to the shadow of all the city. She walked under the El and came to the entrance to the shop. Monday, a new week. Hard beginning, going again to work, heat, fatigue. She entered the building. A man in a white shirt and overalls stood on the stairs, adjusting a ladder. Another man was mixing a can of paint. She could smell the caustic odor from it and from another large can that stood open. The canvas that had been there the week before had been pulled to a new position on the stairs.

As she started upstairs, another girl came in the doorway behind her, and was so close when she reached the door of the shop that she held the door open for her. "Thank you," the girl said. They went inside and she watched the girl go to the long table where she worked. She had noticed her before, her face seemed slightly foreign, possibly Polish. As a child she had known some Polish workers in the town where she lived. The girl's figure was broad and strong, like theirs, but her hair was light. As more girls and women came in, she forgot about her.

Mr. Farbman went among the girls and women saying, "We got to get out a big order today, Gunther's—" The work began with a hard sound quickening minute by minute until it was soon identical with that of every other day. Irons, sewing machines, needles, the racket and heat of work. She knew that the dresses would soon begin to pile up and that she, like the others, would have to work faster, searching seam after seam, cutting the threads, lifting, pushing.

She had thought that after Sunday and its rest she would not feel so tired, but as the morning went on, she began to feel as tired as before. The day was hot and very soon she began to notice something; it was a peculiar smell. What?—then she remembered. The painters at work in the hall; the odor of the paint was beginning to come into the shop. Its peculiar smell, as it became stronger, was nauseating; it hurt her eyes. Turpentine. She had always been susceptible to odors. The girls and women were restless and looked up irritably from their work. The air of the shop had never been good; now it became unbearable. Each breath became an effort of will; she retched with paint. Specks of blackness revolved along the walls, sweat formed and ran down her face. She cut, breathed, tasted turpentine, cut, cut. Suddenly, almost without knowing what was happening, she fell forward...

The girl for whom she had opened the door in the morning held her, holding her head down, and wiped her forehead with a wet handkerchief. "There," she said in a low voice, "that's better. You'll be all right in a minute." She moved to get up and the girl supported her around the shoulders; work in the room was going on as usual. Nauseated but no longer faint, she stood up and went back to work. Although the faintness did not return, the constant taste of the turpentine and paint at every breath she drew sickened her. At last she went to the lavatory and vomited; when she came back, she felt weaker but less sick.

The rest of the morning she worked as well as she could; she was able to keep up with the dresses. She examined a dress about every four minutes. Her stomach felt hollow, as it had been the night on the subway, the moment just before she had left the train. The El roared outside. She worked on by will, without thought.

At twelve o'clock, a number of girls and women got up to leave. The girl who had held her when she fainted came to her and said, "How are you feeling now?"

"Better," she said.

She walked downstairs with her. "Places like this are too cheap to have a fan." The girl hesitated. "You're sure you feel better?"

"Yes, I do."

"I've noticed you go home. I'll walk with you, if you want me to."

"That's good of you."

They walked side by side, the girl watching to see that she was all right. Although there was a dry hot feeling in her mouth and her temples ached, she walked steadily. The El shadows dropped bars on them, running across her eyes; it was a fence. Fence. She glanced at the girl beside her. It had been good of her to help her. She remembered her arm around her shoulders; she was strong. Gentle. Her face belonged in the country, not the city. High strong cheekbones, almost a Polish peasant face. Intelligent. Although the girl had fair hair, her eyes were dark. The El shadows poured across them, ran their bars down the face, the full breasts, the strong figure. "Have you worked at the shop long?" she said.

"Quite a while. Nine months."

Somewhat awkwardly, they began to talk to each other. The girl apparently wanted to be friendly. In her voice was a fullness, a depth of sympathy that reminded her of Miss Child. Even deeper in resonance, the breath, the throat strong. A cloud covered the sun; the shadows disappeared leaving a momentary half-light. She had told the girl that she was married, that her husband worked. "He doesn't make very much, though." "Who does?" the girl said. She said she lived at home, that her father was not working. He had had a job until two years ago. As the girl said it, she felt she was trying to conceal her emotion; she was too evidently matter of fact. They turned the street corner into her street and came to the gate beside the stable. All at once she realized that nobody had yet come through this gate with her except John. Now she was bringing a friend with her, who would see where she lived. It pleased her; it was a proof of her possession. They went through the narrow passageway out into the courtyard—the sun was shining again; the front of the house caught its sidewise light so that the door and windows looked as though cut out with a saw. A cloud floated above the roof. The girl looked up, face dark, her eyes hemmed in by houses. Again the feeling that she belonged in the country, that she was out of place here, in the city. They went inside, up the dark stairway to her room; it had only a glint of sun now, was warm and close. Her room. "It's hot. You ought to have some air," the girl said. She went to a window and opened it. "How nice," she said. She looked around the room, "I wish to God—" suddenly she stopped. Her eyes were embarrassed, as if she had said something she wanted not to say, "Would you forgive me if I asked you something?" "Yes." "Do you love your husband?" "Yes, I do, very much." Looking away, the girl said, "And you're happy?" "Yes, I am." Still not looking at her, the girl said, "I'm in love with a man, he loves me, but—we can't get married." "Why not?" The girl said that her father was out of work, other things—five in the family living in a small flat, a younger brother, the reasons of poverty. "What about the man you're in love with?" "Al? He doesn't make much. But the main thing is my own family. My sister and I work; we keep the family going. Except for that, Al and I would take a chance." "If you knew it, you really ought to be happy—" "Why!" the girl said. "Because, if something happened—I mean sometime, you know at least you can get married." The girl looked at her with a peculiar look. "But you are married," she said. "You—" Harriet saw the mistake; she couldn't know. She had been cruel. "I—I was thinking of somebody I knew who can never marry the man she loves." "Oh," the girl said.

Harriet suddenly felt faint, her head fell forward; the girl sprang to her side. "Forgive me," she said. "Oh, what have I done! I shouldn't have told you all this. I ought to be letting you rest." She helped her to the bed and made her lie down. "I'm a fool, a fool. What can I get you? Is there some soup or something I can warm for you?" "Yes." The girl went to the kitchen and opened a can of soup for her; feeling better, she sat up on the edge of the bed and drank it. "How about you?" she said. "I don't need anything. Sometimes I go without my lunch." "Shouldn't we be going back?" "Rest a little longer. They can stand it for once if we're late." She thought of the shop, the heat, the smell of turpentine. If she were only able to get through this one day. She lay back on the bed again and said to the girl, "What's your name?"

"Anna Tannik."

"Mine is Harriet Kohler."

19

THAT NIGHT when John came home, he said, "You look sick. What's the matter with you?" "I had a bad day." She had her hands over her eyes; they were burning. "Is something wrong with your eyes?" "Yes," she said. "They're doing some painting. The turpentine got in my eyes."

"I want you to drop that job," he said.

"No," she said.

She lay down; he got supper ready. "John," she called. He came to the kitchen door. "It isn't so bad. I made friends with a girl in the shop." He said nothing and went back. Apparently he was angry with her. But he was good, good to let her lie down, breathing the turpentine out of her lungs, forgetting the nine hours past and the next day to come. But she thought, Perhaps she ought to stop, to be able to work for him again as a woman. But there was more to it than working for him, than being a woman. She lay with her arms outstretched; she was so tired that her arms and legs hurt. Her eyes were hot, at moments scalding. If she were not so tired, perhaps the turpentine would not have affected her so. The early darkness of the room, its quiet, touched her with its usual peace. The shop was not everything. When she was there, the long hours and monotony covered, swallowed up all time. But peace was waiting; it was the room, John; it was more than rest and sleep. Dearer, more real because of her work. When supper was ready, she got up and went into the kitchen; John turned and took her in his arms.

"So you made friends with a girl?" he said as they sat down.

"Yes, one of the girls who works at the long table—"

"Yes?"

"Her name is Anna Tannik."

"What is she like?" She told him with some enthusiasm about Anna; she said nothing about her fainting. When she had described her, she said, "Do you think she could be Polish?" "Quite likely," he said. She told him about Anna's family, about how she could not get married. "Her father has been out of work for two years. But he's a good worker, Anna said."

"It doesn't mean anything."

"He'd been working ten years in the place where he was last."

"It still doesn't mean anything. In the machine shops, men with twenty-five years in one place are fired." When they were through eating, she said she wanted to clean up as usual, but he refused. "No, I'll do the work tonight. You rest." She sat back in her chair and closed her eyes which still smarted; through her eyelids the electric bulb of the kitchen glowed, a shaking universe. "This turpentine," he said as he worked. "It's a shame there's no fan, no ventilation in your place. The same thing in the machine shops. Only there they use cyanide; the fumes are poison. Vogel, I think I've mentioned him to you, had cyanide poisoning several years ago." Vogel, a grinder he had spoken to her about; he sometimes described the men at the shop.

20

THE NEXT day she was stronger, and the paint, which had dried somewhat, gave off less turpentine. What still remained of it, its rasping smell brought back some of the nausea of the day before, and coated her throat. But she was not sick, she was able to work; the heat fortunately was more moderate, as the weather was cloudy and turned to rain.

Anna spoke to her when she came in, and asked her how she felt. One or two other girls spoke to her too—one the Negro girl who had spoken to her before. The work began; faces receded, the shop became blank again. Yet she felt a sense of being part of a group, and through Anna and the few girls she had spoken to she too began to reach out to this group. She began to feel the shop as its people, to respond to it, through working in it.

As the week slowly passed, she began to become inured to hard labor. It seemed strange to her that she had ever sat down most of the day, that in fact her whole previous life had been largely that of sitting down. Now the single act of standing up, once endured and become habitual, seemed at least equally natural. She had not imagined she had so much strength in her body.

The second day after she had fainted, instead of going home for lunch, she went to eat with Anna and two other girls. Like them, she brought a lunch, and they went to a small delicatessen with a lunch counter and bought five cent bottles of milk. As it was crowded, she and Anna sat together and the other two girls found a separate place. Friendship between herself and Anna. It was something she could not explain to herself; although they were different and knew it, they liked each other, reached out to each other. As they ate, Anna told her more about her father, and she recognized that this was something she would not have done with anybody, that it was an intimate confidence only for her.

"My father is getting broken—I don't know how to tell you. When somebody like him has been used to working, it does something to them not to work. Something gets weak. It isn't that he doesn't try to get work. Nobody could try harder than he does. He walks miles and miles—to save carfare, going wherever he gets any idea there's work. But thousands do the same thing. He knows we don't blame him, but something is getting weakened. He doesn't sleep, he says things that hurt us. 'I'm no good,' he says, or, 'I take your money.'" She paused. "You know, he might do something—"

Around them were the marble slabs, the racks of cracker boxes, the food bins, of the delicatessen. They could see faces past the racks and shadows and dirt.

"My father says the firm he worked for didn't really have to fire him. But by firing a few men, they could make the men they kept work harder." Mr. Tannik's job had been making cigars. "I'd worry more about him," Anna said, "but he has something that's keeping his courage up. Maybe it won't come through, but a relative in Cleveland has written he may be able to get him into a place there in the fall."

"I hope he does!"

When they finished eating, they went out to the street to get some air before going back to the shop. Anna said, "I live over an El. I never seem to get away from it."

The shop became increasingly familiar and her work in a sense easier. Yet there were times of exhaustion, when sweat and soreness were almost as hard as at the beginning and the monotonous hours passed slowly. John said once, "How long are you going to keep this job?" "I need it," she said. It had grown to mean something to her, a proof of herself. The scissors, the pinking machine, the heat, the faces, the roar of sound made up a new way of life, solid, filling her hours between night and night. This was what she had wanted when she had looked for work before. Now it helped her, not as much as it could have then, but it helped.

A week later, she noticed there was less work than usual; the pace of the shop had let down slightly. It was not much, but she felt a little less driven, there was a less concentrated and body wracking movement in the work. Women, girls who had hardly ever lifted their eyes from the table, whose hands were continually in motion, now paused and looked at each other, talked to each other. The designer smoked indolently as he worked.

Anna said to her, "This Saturday, mark my word, he'll fire somebody, maybe several—orders must be dropping off." She added, "Unless he's expecting more work next week."

"Is that what usually happens?" she said.

"Yes, that's what happens."

"Has it happened often before?"

"Oh, not for four or five months. He's had a good run."

On Saturday she saw Mr. Farbman glancing at her; she had an idea of what was on his mind. At five o'clock, as the others were leaving, he said, "I'd like to speak to you a minute." He turned to speak to another girl. She saw Anna hesitate at the door, waiting for her, almost as though she knew what was going to be said. Mr. Farbman turned to her. "I'm very sorry," he said, "I won't need you next week. You're a good worker, but things is slowing up and I'm gonna put Miss Freedman on your job. She needs the job; she's been here longer and can do other work. I understand you're married—"

"Yes."

"Your husband working?"

"Yes," she said.

"Well, it may be kinda hard on you, but you can stand it—"

She said nothing.

"If things pick up—"

Anna met her at the door. "Did he let you out?" she said.

"Yes."

"I was afraid that would happen. He doesn't waste any time."

The newly painted stairway ahead shifted to darkness, to emptiness. John, the house; this cutaway feeling was not without help. But she felt that a part of her strength was being taken from her.

Anna walked along under the El with her.

"We'll still see each other," she said. "Is it going to be very tough for you?"

"No, not so bad. Not the money."

Anna said nothing, asked no explanation of her.

"Come over to the house next week," Harriet said.

"All right."

They stopped at the foot of the El station where Anna took the train home. Newspapers flapped in a stand beside them. She thought with regret that she would no longer see Anna at the long table, her face sideways to her, usually preoccupied and tight with work, but occasionally lifted so that their glances met. And it was not just Anna. It was the shop itself, the movement, the sound of machines and work. It was the equal relationship of work into which she had been allowed to enter. Sweating and aching, she had found in it more satisfaction than she had ever had before.

Anna talked with her for a moment and then went upstairs to take the El.

She walked away feeling again, in spite of the room ahead, the emptiness of being jobless. She was being thrown towards some vacancy she feared.

21

JOHN HELD her arm. They were walking west, along a dark street that smelled of the river.

Night. Salt dark, life. And death thrown large, on the screen of the houses—yet, shadow? Had sleep, strength yet. Three days, since she had lost her job—it was a different peace, less sure? Street lamps. Anna. The faces of the moving thread, the sewing machines. She had needed the oppression, but they had not. Had needed work, even with oppression. But they had not. A 10¢ movie house, black script "IS THERE A PRICE OF FAME TOO HIGH FOR A WOMAN TO PAY? A Drama of—" A man stared at it, hands in pockets. Spindles, hours, thread drawing its slow line across their temples. The night was deep in every cross street and ahead in the sky meeting the city. Roofs. They had seen the glow of the sun striking up its afterlight, like a geranium in a pot. Restlessness. Or did the river whisper to them? He said, "How would you like a ferry ride." At a bend in the street a small iron railing; behind it there were several sunken graves. In several streets she had seen these graveyards left aside by time—how deep the shadows were, a night, a grass of blackness. Brother, what's here, death? this blackness where light ends. John stopped and they leaned on the iron railing, looking at silence on the stones. Two shadows. "Is now sleep" but never sky, never stars. You have wept there, it is the place of your. He took her hand, covered it. Her mind held to his hand, its strength. Must not remember. Ahead an elevated railroad track, in black steel, and beyond it the West Side Elevated Highway. They walked on. "The body of" saw a sailor lying in a cement recess. Darkened crotch, he had urinated; the line ran unevenly to the street. "this death." Fatigue, she had used it to forget. "Special, Spring Flowering Bulbs: Bartigan, Keizerkroon, Couronne d'Or, 60 to 85¢ a dozen." At last they turned the corner and walked along the docks. The numbers, digits under the roofs, implied the mass of ships; where did they lie? A taxi passed. They crossed the wide street to the ferry house and entered the waiting room. Now the river, the smell of the sea. After silence, the thunder of shoved water came; the piles shook. They walked down into the night, saw the moon at their knees; over the side the water lapped their shadows. When? Another shadow. Remember. Not sun now but the beading path of the moon, the sun's reverse. Dead. Had he died? less light; the ferry slip rolled and sighed with the sea. In the interior of the boat a gong sounded and the platform of the waves began slowly to go under them. Their shadows moved faster, licked crests of night. She looked up the wide avenue of the river, away from the sea. Each wave was a noose; the pistons' throb held, steady, scissors raining threads on the floor. Anna, the spindles infinite as the delay of love. Yet you are alive. "Yet if you knew it, you should be happy." In its cloudy center, the sky. The engines hesitated, she wanted only to hear the sound of the sea. The windows of the empty cabins lit it, it passed under them and was gone. Silence of wind, "How do you like it?" John said. He was leaning against a life preserver; as he spoke, a horse snuffled. The stable. "I like it." This was slowness, the meaning of night; in their wake, a barge passed, holding a staff of lights—voice sounded "is made of coal." Mines, blackness, slate, air. Earth or sea, it was an equal death. At a change in the engine throb, she saw that they were approaching shore. Thrashing barriers. Again the blow on the piles, the reversal of the screws and chain roar. She looked upward. Two upper balconies were dark, two gangplanks vacant in the night. Held where? to what shore STOP LOOK there was a cobbled entry ahead. "Shall we walk around?" Up past the wheel, hanging chains, tired curve of trolley trestle. 35¢. A Night. Railhead destinations of America, Scranton Chicago on cloth. Beyond the tracks it became quieter and they were alone at the edge of the water, on a thick beam. They could hear the suck of the water, as soft as horses' lips. A culvert from the river, six black tugs, dark, their thick sides expanding and contracting.

"Stay here," she said. "Stay here, John." They stood a long time without moving, looking at the tugs, the night, and the endless dark lap of the water.

22

THEY WERE to visit Anna. Anna had told her where she lived, a flat in a building over stores on Columbus Avenue, what station on the El to get off at. 110th. "Walk back." Near the Park, but blocks of roofs, airless. Anna had said, "It might do my father good to see somebody."

They had not yet met Albert, the man Anna was going with. John had met Anna, and liked her. He said she reminded him of a cousin he had in the West and added, "I saw what you were telling me about. It was hard for her, seeing us." The same look, watching until she forgot.

The day before the visit, after supper, John asked her if she wanted to go out. "No, not particularly," she said. "Come on—" he said, and pulled her to her feet. She looked at him questioningly; she always humored him when he wanted her to, knowing that he would humor her in return. They went out into the street and walked towards a main street of stores nearby. The lights shone in many of the store windows; few of them closed early in this neighborhood. At a store with women's dresses draped in the window, John stopped and said, "Let's go in here." Surprised, she went in with him, yet hesitating to enter this store that looked like a private room. Around the sides were racks of dresses and she thought how much they looked like the racks of dresses in the shop where she had worked. And yet not the same. Perhaps the models were a little different, or the arrangement on the racks. As they stood near the entrance of the shop, a girl came up to them. "Can I help you?" she said.

"Yes," John said. "I'd like to get my wife a dress."

She almost started to say no.

"Had you anything in particular in mind?" the girl said, speaking half to John and half to Harriet.

A little embarrassed, John said, "I saw a dress in the window a few days ago, it was yellow and had some buttons—"

"Along the shoulders?"

"Yes, that was the one."

The girl ran her hand down a rack of dresses and pulled one out. "Is that it?"

"Yes, that's it."

"What size do you wear?" she said, turning to Harriet, "about a sixteen?"

"Yes," she said; she knew nothing about sizes.

The girl got out the dress and said, "Would you like to try it on?"

John nodded for her.

"There's a dressing room in here."

She took the dress and went in, into a clean-smelling cubicle. Taking her old dress off, she stretched up her arms and let the new dress fall in a torrent over her, shook her arms into it, and when it was on, fastened three snap buttons at the side. The dress clung to her cleanly; she saw that it was becoming. And yet she thought of how it had been made, of the seams, that some girl like herself might have sewn, examined, and she heard the click of needles, the pounding of the iron; there returned to her all the heat, the limitless fatigue of the shop. Her hands went quickly to the buttons at her side, and yet she hesitated. John wanted to give her the dress; it would mean a great deal to him. And with workers of all kinds it must be the same; a miner hated coal, other workers hated what they made . . . Adjusting the dress, she opened the door of the cubicle and went out.

At once she could see that John was pleased, that the way the dress looked on her satisfied him. "Wear it," he said. He looked around. "Is there anything else you want?"

On a small counter by the door was a display of pocketbooks. She remembered the night on the subway and the two girls, holding their pocketbooks. If she had a pocketbook, confidence? Strength for her hands?

"I'd like a pocketbook," she said.

23

THE NEXT night, they took the train to 110th Street, and getting off, rode down to the street in a slow elevator. To the east, dark shrubbery moved by the night wind; "That's Central Park," John said. They turned and followed the El back. Over a small park to the north was the bulk of a group of buildings olive black, streaked with apparent arches— "What's that?" she said. "Up there? The Cathedral of St. John the Divine." "Could we go up and see it?" "Yes, if you want to." They walked up the park edge, past posts and railings. Below them lights, white yellow globes in the park, were just beginning to glow. Slowly the horizon to the east lengthened the limit of the avenues, where the sky dragged humidly to night. "There are so many people in the city," she said. Under roofs, lives eastward. They looked up at the Cathedral; people walked up and down, and its heavy walls, fenced away, were cold, high, the crosses on all the dark buttress chapels distant, archaic, and stiff. Steps that should be for entrance came down in slabs to no path; a few small trees refused their elbows to the stone. They passed the rear chapels and turned west along one side. A heavy dome, the heavy unshaped mass aloof over the park from the city poor; contractors' sheds; tombs of the dead saints. "This is my body which is broken" but not for the street. At Amsterdam Avenue, the nave end, they looked up over the Gothic doorways where a metal framework fell, thin over the upper stone. Its lattices rode clouds: louder than stone, they were corridors for the feet of workmen. As they walked away, towards 110th, she said, "Do you make scaffoldings?" "No," he said. "It's not a

lathe job. It's just made from pipe sections clamped together."
"It's beautiful," she said.

They went down 110th again to Columbus Avenue, to the high
curve of the El, and turned south under it. The structure filled the
street, its diagonal struts under the track, its heavy posts repeating the angle of the moon. The odd numbers which they wanted
were on the east side of the street; they went along store fronts
looking for the building GRUESOME MURDER of prices, an
anatomy of the heart, stomach, kidneys "use in all cases of continued nervousness, head-aches, pains of the back" LION BREW-
ERY. Beyond the store signs the El structure, there was something
free about the street, a width of space in which children played.
Darkness, these voices, the sound almost of their own street.

"I guess this is it," John said, looking at a gilt number in a glass
doorway between two stores. They looked for letterboxes, but the
row of usual house boxes had long since been staved in, only a few
twisted metal doors remaining, with no names. "You said they
were on the fourth floor, didn't you?" John said. "Yes." As the
door was open, they went in along a long corridor leading to a
stairway. The steady wailing of a baby could be heard—ah, ah,
ah, ah, ah, ah, ah. Why did a baby's voice penetrate so? "Go ahead
up," John said. A strangling faint smell of really sour wood. The
stairs had a carpet runner on them, fastened by a strip of metal at
each tread; the carpet was colorless with dirt. Shadows. To their
left windows at intervals gave on a dark airshaft, across which
they could see the lighted windows of flats in the next building.
Shaft of night. At the landing of the second floor was a littered
backless alcove with baby carriages in it; nearby stood an empty
garbage can with the lid off, there were scraps of garbage where
another can had stood. Going towards the front to the next flight
of steps, they heard a dull roar and a light appeared through a
frosted transom and faded, the passing of the El train outside.
The El, its sound, its light, continually beating at this house. She
remembered one trip alone on the El, windows seen from outside,

curtains, beds. Now inside, now across the darkness, a room, the long flowing of the train.

At last they reached the fourth floor and knocked on a door. In a moment Anna opened it, as if she had been waiting for them, and said, "Hello, Harriet. Hello, John. Come in"; she took Harriet's hand. Behind her, as they went in, they saw another girl. "This is my sister, Rowe," Anna said. Rowe was smaller than Anna, a fresh, delicate-looking girl. Going through a narrow hallway, they entered a living room, a bare clean room with windows on a rear courtyard. Standing near one window was a man of middle height, his shoulders curved and lax. He had a dark moustache and looked foreign. "This is my father," Anna said. "Father, this is my friend Harriet and her husband, John Kohler." "Glad to meet you, Mr. Kohler," Mr. Tannik said. "And this is my mother," Anna said. A small plain-faced woman held out her hand to them. Rowe called, "Herb!" A boy came out of an adjoining bedroom. "This is Herb," Rowe said, "the baby of the family." "Get a couple of chairs from the kitchen," Anna said. Herb and Rowe got the chairs and they all sat down.

"Did you have trouble finding us?" Anna said.

"No, none at all," Harriet said. "We got off the El at 110th Street and from what you said John knew about where it was." She said John knew the city better than she did.

"You haven't been here so long?" Mrs. Tannik said to Harriet.

"No."

"My girls and boy they're born here."

The windows on the courtyard had white curtains, hanging motionless. The courtyard was hardly larger than the airshaft they had seen; across it were the lighted windows of another building. There seemed to be no air, the atmosphere inside and out was close, heated.

"Take off your coat, Mr. Kohler," Mrs. Tannik said. "Be comfortable."

He took off his coat and hung it over the back of his chair.

Harriet, sitting beside him, leaned against his shoulder. Mrs. Tannik spoke of the weather. "It's been so warm," she said. "We all feel it, especially Rowe."

Rowe made a face. "Everybody feels the heat."

"Rowe is my delicate child." She spoke of Rowe's childhood, with the pleasure of speaking of the past, the good time? Her husband, too, spoke once, but hesitantly. In this room, with cracked bare walls, the faint but pervading smell of tenement filth, the closeness and the heat, Harriet felt a sudden terror: a life seen backward, the past its only meaning. As Mr. Tannik spoke, his face had a boyish look; as he became silent, it faded. The side-wise stiff look of age, the look of defeat.

There was a knock on the hallway door and Anna went to open it. She came back with a young man who was evidently expected, and said to Harriet and John, "This is Al. I told him you were coming. Al, this is Harriet and this is John Kohler." Al shook hands with both of them. He had a firm grip, he was young but already had lines in his face. He sat down by Anna and remained quiet, as if he were often part of the family circle.

Mrs. Tannik said, "You should have been here, Al. We were talking about Rowe."

"He'd rather hear about Anna," Rowe said.

The children and mother began talking among themselves. After a moment, Mr. Tannik leaned over to John and said, "What kind of work you do, Mr. Kohler?"

"I work in a machine shop, run a lathe."

"I used to work in a cigar factory. I have no work in two years, though. Makes it hard."

"It must."

"You don't know of anything, anything at all, do you?"

"No, I can't say I do. There's nothing at the shop I work at. They let two men go a month ago."

Mr. Tannik's face became drawn. "I been trying for months, everywhere, and that's what I hear. I can't understand—" He stopped. "I got a relative in Cleveland. He thinks maybe he can get me on in a factory there in the fall. He says things are gonna pick up."

"I hope—"

Mrs. Tannik had been listening, over the conversation of her children. "If you don't get that job, something else will come along, George," she said.

The talk went on, leaving Mr. Tannik by himself, silent. Harriet thought of what a good man he seemed to be, of how if he were working, he would enter into the talk, of how he would be different, full of life. "Life." She saw with him the broken plaster of the wall, many renovations cheaply done. Cheapness, poverty. Unknown before, the living in tenements. Airshaft, El. In how many rooms of how many cities? talking "they're tearing down the building on a Hundred Seventh" saw the at least clean rooms, corridors of the hospital "was back again today, wants to buy clothes" here freedom broke the body, the mind "no we have nothing I told him" "I told him but he kept asking" eyes, love and its feared result, conception "you used to say that, Al. Don't you remember?" children coming growing. She was outside, to find freedom "meat you paid eighteen cents a pound for six months ago" "thirty cents now" curtains and radios, "life." "They say the processing tax—" Mr. Tannik sat silent, said nothing.

Speaking over several conversations, Mrs. Tannik said, "It's so hot, Anna; we have some iced tea in the icebox—see if we have enough to serve." "Yes, we have enough," Anna said, going into the kitchen. "It isn't very cold," she called. "The ice is almost gone." Harriet and Rowe went in to help her serve it. They used five glasses of different sizes and three cups; Anna apologized for not having a complete set. "They keep breaking and—" The tea was cool enough, tasted good, but the heat and closeness of the night poured back; sweat came on Al's and Mr. Tannik's foreheads. "Is it getting hotter? You're positively sweating," Anna said to Al and ran her finger over his forehead. "Mr. Kohler's the only one who's standing the heat." "I work near a welding furnace," he said. "Let's go up on the roof," Anna said. "At least we'll have some air." "Can you go up on the roof?" Harriet said. "Yes, there's a stairway to it."

They went out in the hall and started up. Loud voices came from behind one or two doors—in a half-drunken argument "I say thash not true what—" faded below them. "Go careful here," Anna said. The stairs became narrower and at the top Anna slowly shoved back a metal-covered door that scraped along the roof. Out of the blackness of the airshaft a shadow of sky, air cooling and fresher. They all pushed through the door out to the roof, to its quiet and dark. Radio aerials ran lines from walls to chimneys, stringing space; they felt the size of night. Parapets bordered the roof and the airshaft, and with shadowed vents and chimneys, kept them from the pull of earth. Below them, in geometric tiers, were other parapeted roofs which held not so much moonlight as the city's light reflected downward from the sky. The sky had no night; pale in the center, it rayed to a nervous horizon which threshed with electric signs. Continually loud, El trains passed throwing flares of blue sparks. Harriet looked for the Cathedral; it appeared to the north, its latticed scaffolding thin in the distance. Turning, she looked for Mr. Tannik.

Mr. Tannik, by himself, stood at the edge of the parapet looking down.

24

THE FOLLOWING morning she finished the housework and looked out the open window. Stable, the courtyard, everything known and quiet. Peace, but yet not peace. She thought of Anna's father walking tiredly somewhere. Al, the lines of his face. She leaned on the edge of the window frame and shook her black hair out of her eyes. Light absorbed the night before; voices ended in the usual sounds; peace denied and yet did not deny the remembered form of the city.

Half an hour later she went downstairs. She wanted to feel around her the kingdom of the children which was a partial freedom, away from the life of men. She paused at the outer gate and looked through its metal, the sun putting lozenges on her skin. With this barrier between her and the street, she felt the physical separateness between her and childhood; she put her fingers to it. Yet as she looked, it disappeared; her sight went through it.

She went outside. Slowly she walked up and down the street, stepping over some broken boards the children had left, passing entrances to laundries or driveways back into buildings or yards. She watched the children as they played, active, never tired, in groups up and down the street, some at games she could not even understand. Two small children sat slapping each other. They gave each other slow slaps, in turn; nobody noticed them. They seemed happy.

No hallways had doors, or doors closed. The children went in and out, the littlest ones hitching themselves up by holding on railings, and disappearing in inside doors or up unpainted stairs.

As she passed one doorway, she saw through a short hall in the building what looked like a rear courtyard. As there seemed to be no privacy, she went in and crossing the hall, came out in the back. She saw a bare flagstone court, fifteen feet square, shadowed and enclosed by surrounding buildings. Overhead were fire escapes and sagging lines of clothes; on one line, baby clothes, on another, workingmen's shirts, overalls, underwear, and women's underthings. Across from the door she had come through was another door. As she stepped into the middle of the yard, a girl of ten or twelve, olive-skinned, came wandering out of the door across from her. She sat down unconcernedly on a wooden box and stared upwards, not appearing to notice her. Suddenly, as though speaking her thoughts, she said, "Do you know Rosalie?"

"No."

"I like her." The girl clasped her hands over one knee. "I can't talk to her, though."

"Why not?"

"Oh, I can't; none of us can."

"Why?"

"She's married and her husband doesn't believe. So she isn't going to heaven."

"Oh, I'm sure she is."

"No, I know. They won't let her."

"Why not?"

"Because of her husband. If she left her husband, it would be all right."

"So do you want her to?"

"Yes."

The girl drew a stocking up, and her lovely arms again supported her knee. "Where is heaven," she said.

"Don't you know?"

"In the sky?"

"No."

"Where?"

But Harriet said nothing.

The girl unclasped her knee, the two lines of her arms that had been tense breaking. She looked at her and said, "Tell me."

"No." After a pause, Harriet said, "What's your name?"

"Mary."

"I hope I'll see you again. Do you live here?"

"Yes."

Somewhere inside one of the buildings a voice called and the girl jumped up and ran away; Harriet walked slowly home.

25

A HURDY-GURDY was grinding in the early evening; the darkness was only distantly coming. She had just finished the supper dishes, and was standing in the front room at the window with John. Sound, color; she felt happy.

"Let's go out, John," she said.

"All right."

When they were in the outside air, the evening had a special light, a tone of yellow turned nakedly along the streets. In such a light, although beautiful, the immediacy of the world was threatening. Even now, even after the months with John, it was threatening.

As they were going down the street, she touched John's arm. "Do you see that child over there, that girl?"

"Yes."

"That's Mary, the one I was telling you about."

"Pretty child."

They passed her without her noticing them, and turned the corner. Into the world of pushcarts, Italian papers. "*Uomo ucciso e abbandonato in un' automobile, vincino la corsa dei 6 giorni al Garden.*" Always "*la morte*"—cross in the church, the city's sorrow. The face of the child Mary was all these faces and her eyes their eyes.

They walked on, away from the street into another street. The light began to fade slowly from the buildings, leaving the first blur of darkness. With the loss of twilight, she felt the world less real. John said, "How about a movie?" They had been a few times to movies together, to cheap theaters. "All right," she said, glad he had suggested going. They went into a place under the El offering a feature and a western. The outside was plastered solid with posters, stills from the movies being shown; a few children hung around the entrance, watched irritatedly by the ticket collector. They looked longingly at John and her going in.

As they went into the darkness of the theater, which had no balcony but just a double row of wooden seats down to the screen, she thought of the hall at the hospital, somewhat the same, where the weekly movie was shown. She had gone every week; it was a way of reaching the outside world, of escaping the hospital. Dark too, escape from sight. "Here," John said. There were two seats off the aisle and they edged in to them. "Can you see all right?" he said. "Yes." They settled down into the hard wooden seats and John, after a moment's hesitation, put his arm around her. Only men in front of them, worn hard faces looking intently at the screen; the western was being shown; several cowboys in what was apparently a ranch bunkhouse were singing. At a signal from their leader, they got up, and with hands pressed into wide belts, walked out into open space. It was outside that she became lost, in the flat grass flowing with sun. The sound, the clop of hooves; they had mounted horses. She hardly understood what was happening, seeing only the sun, the space, the glide and streaming of perpetual light. Buck Jones, sun across his guns. She laid her head on John's shoulder; her hair touched his cheek. The theater was returning again—with her eyes better fitted to the dark, she could see all the faces, each tight-lipped jaw, flare of nostril. Men, the male odor, tobacco dusk.

A new feature was beginning. Gradually she realized she was seeing the office of a prison warden. A prisoner was being brought in. Movement of shadows, bodies against walls. Fadeout and along her expanding blood, camera into step step advance to key and lock, cell. Time and walking to the "shop," working, the whispering of hope. Plan to break jail. Desperate slow hours, the waiting, planning. Her fingers closed over the seat edge; rasp of a saw, shadows. A cell door opened; the guard was taken. Other doors opening, the mob agony, uncertainty, pressing forward. Hope now, striped suits crawling along a wall, dropping forward. Rush to the outer wall; alarm, guns. At the last wall, only one got free; the rest were driven back. Sirens moaned into the night. John said, "All right?" "Yes." "Want to go out?" "No." She wanted to be sure the prisoner escaped. Beyond this, nothing. She watched with unintermitted anxiety until she knew, and then saw the dark again, the gaunt faces around her. Her blood slowed; they got up and left the theater. In the street, the world became solid and took its accustomed form; the buildings were dark and the neon light was flickering along the avenue.

26

JOHN, AFTER his first conversation with her, had not spoken to her often about the mines. Once, when her elbow had opened a gas jet accidentally and enough gas had escaped to fill the kitchen with its disagreeable odor, he had mentioned the smell of gas in the mines. "The most dangerous gas you couldn't smell," he said. And he had described the precautions they took to test the air for gas. Although he seldom spoke of the mines, she knew they existed for him, were a dark memory in him. She could see the particular look in his eyes when he received a letter from his brother, Jimmy, as he had twice since the early summer. These letters spoke of hardship, debts, lack of steady work—they were not complaining; whether Jimmy had mentioned these difficulties or not, he would have known about them. "No miner ever gets his head above water," he said. When he sensed that things were going particularly hard with his brother, he sent him money.

A week after he had sent him one such remittance, he received a letter of thanks which, to her surprise, disturbed him. His brother said that he was going to go to a new mine, still in the same state, where he could make more money. He gave the address where future letters should be sent to him: c/o Cordoba Mining Corporation, Gannettsville, Ohio.

"That Cordoba mine doesn't sound so good," John said.

"Why?" she asked.

"I know that mine and there's only one reason why it would pay more money than the place where Jim is now."

"What's that?"

"They must be robbing pillars."

"What does that mean?"

"It means they're giving a man twenty per cent more money and raising his risks a thousand per cent; here, I'll show you." Robbing pillars, he said, was one of the most dangerous jobs in coal mining; it was done in a particular type of mine, like the Cordoba mine, where the vein of coal covered a hill. In such a mine, a level tunnel was cut through the vein all around the bottom of the hill; from this tunnel the men began digging upwards, in wide cuts, leaving stretches of coal called "pillars" between the cuts. In these pillars there were safety chambers; the men set a blast, then hid in the chambers and when the coal was blown out, it slid down to the bottom of the cut. When the whole hill had been mined and only the pillars were left standing, supporting the roof, the mine owners "robbed the pillars"; they paid extra money to miners to break the pillars out working from the top down. At some point in the work, the roof caved in, frequently catching the men.

"What about timbering?" she said.

"No good. Not in those mines. Timbers three, four feet thick would be crushed to splinters."

"Then is that what he's doing?"

"Probably—when he says he's getting more money. I don't like it."

He wrote to his brother and asked him if he were robbing pillars. Jimmy wrote back that he was, but it was "near the top" and "wasn't dangerous yet." When it got worse, he promised to quit. John said, "That's what they all say." He wrote urging his brother to give up the job as soon as possible.

27

ONE EVENING Anna was coming to see them, if possible bringing Al. After supper, Harriet straightened up, with particular care, both the kitchen and the front room. Hers. Remembered the first time she had brought Anna to the room, the knowledge of possession. Yet not hers—theirs. John. She looked at him as he sat under the light reading the evening paper. He turned a page; the rustle entered her like a memory. "Your hair needs combing," she said. "All right, you comb it," he said. She made him sit up straight and took his comb and pulled his dark hair over his forehead, making a part with the comb and her hands; she pressed the darkness of his hair away from his eyes. Eyes dark too—from the light overhead, lines of shadow appeared that emphasized his cheek bones. "Your cheeks look more hollow than usual," she said. "You've been tired lately."

"Yes, we've had to work harder," he said.

"How?"

"Oh, the company's lowered the bids on certain jobs; they have to speed up, to make a profit."

"It's a shame!"

"It's the usual thing—"

She took his hands and looked at them. The callouses, she thought, were getting thicker, formed from months of a certain movement; they were stained with oil and dirt. She put one of his hands to her lips, touching its hard surface. Hands of doctors, smooth hands. Dr. Revlin? His hands were hard. "I like your hands," she said. He stood up and put his arms around her, crushing the air out of her. He was strong, tremendously strong, but she could feel his tiredness too. As he let her go, she said, "I wish you didn't have to work so hard." "You're not the only one," he said.

A few minutes later the gate clanged and she said, "Here's Anna." Anna was alone; leaving him, she ran down and met her on the stairs. "Hello," she said. "Al couldn't come?"

"No. He's working tonight."

"That's too bad. It was good of you to come alone."

"I wanted to."

As Anna came in, for a moment she looked around with the same look she always had, of envy. It was immediately gone. She took off her hat, which was close-fitting and around the edge of which her bright hair curled up tensilely. "Thanks," she said as Harriet took it; then she walked around the room in a preoccupied way. Harriet waited until she sat down, then asked her about the shop. "Things are getting even slower, it's even worse than when you were there," she said. "I don't let myself think whether I'll lose my job or not."

"How are Bernice and Gladys?" These were the two girls who used to go to lunch with them.

"All right. Bernice's sister wants her to go to Washington and she's going to quit. By the way, Sadie, Miss Feldman, was let out."

"How about that colored girl, you know—?"

"Oh, she keeps complaining about her relatives from Florida. I guess more keep coming up all the time."

At that moment some horses began a sudden clatter in the stable outside. "Horses?" Anna said.

"Yes, that's a stable in front."

"It's funny to hear a sound like that in the city."

"Have you ever lived in the country?" John asked.

"Oh everybody's lived in the country some time or other. Haven't you?"

"Oh yes."

"I've only visited in the country," Anna said. "My parents,

though, were country people, peasants I suppose you'd say, before they came to this country."

"What country did they come from?" John said.

"Poland, Russian Poland."

"Were they married there?" Harriet asked.

"No, only after they came to this country. My father had to serve a period of military training in Poland, and he wanted to avoid it. My mother got him a passport in the name of a cousin of hers and he escaped from the barracks and crossed the border. Later he brought my mother to this country, when he could support her."

Harriet thought of Mr. Tannik, and now she felt differently about him. During the few moments she had been looking at him the night they had visited Anna, she had seen what he must have been when he was a young man. It took courage to do what he had done. As though Anna were reading her thoughts, she said, "If my father could find work, he wouldn't be afraid of anything. It's not having work that he can't stand."

Harriet went out to the kitchen and got some cake and glasses of milk. She felt disturbed and could think of nothing to say. From what had been said about Mr. and Mrs. Tannik, she began to think of Anna and Al and at last said, "Anna, really, why couldn't you and Al get married? Couldn't you manage it somehow, have Al come to live with you, help with the rent maybe?"

"No—!"

"Why not?"

"Because—" Anna hesitated. "No—I don't want it that way. Don't you see? there's no room, no privacy. Herb sleeps on a sofa. Then my father— No, I have a different idea about marriage; I want—I don't know what I want, but—" A flush reddened her cheeks. "If two people can't live like human beings—" All of them became silent. The horses stamped again in the stable and Harriet remembered how, early one morning, she had seen a horse driven out of the stable and it had looked tired and had shaken its white head.

28

JOHN HAD just finished eating supper, a meal that she had kept and warmed for him, not knowing what time he would be home. For several days he had worked overtime at the shop, coming home exhausted after an eleven or twelve hour day. Tonight he had been earlier, it was only nine thirty; when he came in, he seemed less tired, but now after eating, tiredness overcame him. He rested his head on his hands—"This overtime is a racket," he said. "If they paid time and a half, it would be all right, but they pay straight time. The idea is to give overtime, then cut the pay so that it takes longer hours to make the same money." He was talking more to himself than to her. She said, "Why don't you go in and lie down?" "No," he said. He liked to stay in the kitchen until she had finished the dishes, even when he was tired. He lay back in his chair, closed his eyes, and rested in complete apathy. Over the sound of the dishes, she felt silence, in the kitchen and in the house. It was an unusual silence; it was broken by a click of a door opened upstairs and Rocco came downstairs with his dog. John said, "That's Rocco—taking his dog out." The dog leaped around Rocco and they heard a yelp of pleasure. "He doesn't get out often, the poor dog." The steps died away; in the returning silence she looked at John. His head on the back of the chair, a peculiar effect of the hard light on his half closed eyes troubled her; she remembered the men who had slept on the public daises in the subway. It could not be good for him to come in so exhausted from work. The two nights before she had made him strip to the waist and sit in a chair in front of the sink, and she had washed

188

him, holding his shoulders and rubbing him front and back with a rough cloth. The rubbing, the warmth, made him feel less tired. Then she had dressed him, like a lazy child, in a clean undershirt and shirt. How long would the night work continue? She remembered what he had said about orders, "Five hundred crankshafts—" Orders had to be filled.

"What's that?" John said. A peculiar whine sounded from the courtyard. He got up and went in the front room; she could see him go from the kitchen's light into the night shadow beyond the door. "It's Rocco's dog," he said, coming back. "He's got him tied up in the courtyard." The dog began to bark; soon the barking came almost without a break. "That racket's fearful," John said. They had heard the dog barking occasionally upstairs, but floor and walls muffled it and in any case it was not like this barking which was short, sharp, yet deep. It penetrated everywhere, a steady, desperate sound. It was too loud; there was something unbearable about it. "He's afraid," she said. "Rocco shouldn't have tied him up like that," John said. He hesitated. "Do you want to go down? Maybe we can do something with him."

They went down to the courtyard; the dog was tied crudely by a rope to the pipe conduit that led to the light burning in back of the stable. As he leaped against the rope, a line of fur was pressed back at his neck. "There, there," John said, "what's the trouble? You don't have to bark like that." The dog only backed away, snarled, and then barked louder. The night echoed the bark. The sound carries a good distance, Harriet thought. "It's no use," John said. "He won't stop till Rocco comes back." They went back into the building; the fury of the dog continued behind them.

About five minutes later they heard the gate clang and the barking of the dog stopped. Rocco, she thought. She waited for the sound of his voice. Instead, there was a different voice and a renewed outburst of barking. She ran to the window; John followed her. Below her in the courtyard stood a policeman; his feet were spread, he was standing in front of the dog with a service revolver in his hand. He moved the gun slowly, following the dog as he leaped against the rope. Suddenly a loud report sounded among the buildings like the backfire of an automobile; the policeman put the gun in his holster and walked away.

Instead of the barking, an impossible silence filled the courtyard, the room; the returning sound of the city drifted against it. She stood staring downward. "John, what—" she said. "What did he do it for?"

"Somebody must have complained."

A faint odor of burned powder, the smoke. A sound of voices.

She went to a chair as sound began to return. Voices, steps. Clang of the gate, the sound of steps; she knew Rocco had come back. He stopped by the dog, then came on into the building; she heard his steps on the stairs. When he knocked on the door, John answered. "I see a your light," Rocco said. He held his cap twisted in his hands. "You know who kill my dog?"

"A policeman."

"But I tie him—I come right back!"

John said, "I know. Some damn—"

"God damn, I come right back," Rocco said.

He looked at his cap, then said goodnight and went up to his room. When he was gone, she went and lay face downward on the bed. Stop. Stop. But she could not stop remembering that then too it had been the silence that had been so terrible, and that he had made no sound.

29

JOHN HAD had a hard week, working every night except Friday—Saturday had been particularly hard; he had not come home until half past ten. On Sunday they slept and lay in bed late, putting off the final moment when they would have to get up. This was their day of freedom, of resting, of being together, now doubly important because of the overtime work John was doing, which not only exhausted him but limited the time they were together. Also today, for some reason she could not explain, she felt a particular need of the peace John's presence gave her.

Because the sun had left the room when they finally got up, it seemed only a short time before the change of light in the afternoon began to give the room its illusion of early darkness. Then looking around her with a sudden restlessness, she said, "Do you want to go out?"

"Where?" he said.

"I don't know—but I'd like to go out."

"All right."

To leave the dark room. The hot sun, shining now across the courtyard on the stable, was still over all the city. She was suddenly afraid of darkness, of the coming night that even this afternoon darkening of the room made her feel. She needed the sun and the sun's space of sky.

They decided to go to Central Park. They had already been there a few times. They took the subway to Columbus Circle, and coming up, met the shaft of the Maine monument with its burning sides, passed it, and entered the park. They walked slowly, in the clear sun that came unweakened through a filter of leaves. Trees. In and out among low hummocks and patches of earth walked pigeons, aloof and nodding their humorlessly mechanical heads. As they approached two pigeons on the sidewalk, they rose with a slate-blue tumult across their knees, lifting a flock of pigeons with them. Upward, into the sun. Iridescent, the pigeons swerved and came to earth again; again the pink feet, four pointed claws ticking among the hummocks and bushes. "Let's sit down," she said. She wanted to watch, to follow the necks nodding with light. There were some with brown necks softening to purple. Others were white, slate-hued. Inquisitive, knowing, full of boldness, they came hungrily closer and closer. Inhabitants of heaven, the sun broken downward among the trees would soon suck them up into the air again.

In a few minutes, they walked on. Crossing a bare earth path they saw a sign: DELIVERY ENTRANCE TO ZOO, and over some trees they saw the zoo's dark buildings to the east. She imagined she could hear from them the restless sounds, the impatient tireless padding of imprisoned animals. "Do you want to go to the zoo?" he said. "No!" she said. They crossed a path and came into a wide cement playground near a high rock crag. Children were laughing, playing, throwing ball, climbing, twelve of them at a time outlined over a crest of stone against sky and clouds. There were swings, children children—a pocket of young life. It hurt her to see it, and yet did not. As they walked across the cement paving, around some glittering bathing basins, she saw a child's red belt on the ground, of patent leather, evidently belonging to a dress, which had come undone in play. The child, she thought, will be scolded when her mother finds the belt is gone. Children, mothers; the defiance of the tomb. If she could have a child, yet: hearing beyond summer the tread of time, never-resting time. "Those hours" the minutes loud with nothingness. She took John's arm and walked with him away from the noise of the children that shut away and cooled even the sun.

They crossed a cinder playing field and an asphalt road dark against bushes and sod beside it, and came up a walk on the west side of the park. What was evidently a bridle path here touched the walk: posted by it was a sign, FOR EQUESTRIANS ONLY, and three smart brown horses with brown riders cantered past, straight and nervous. Seen a moment by bitter eyes, dashing away, gone behind trees and rocks. The people who walked near them were real—servants out for a walk, clerks, men and women, married, children grinding by on roller skates. They went under arbors of bared, bark-stripped logs, clasped in the year-wound tangle of wisteria, its sprays of green jabbing pointed shadows over them. They saw again a flight of pigeons and ahead, like a repetition of it, was the color of the lake. As they came to the lake, they walked down close to the shore where brown ducks were swimming, one raising a webbed orange foot out of the water to scratch its neck, and nibbling with its long dark bill at its wing. She stopped with John to look—the ducks went, suddenly slower or faster, with their mysterious, quiet, unseen propulsion, only slight wakes spreading out behind them. A dog came down to the lake edge and barked; they fled back in a circle, protesting with a bitter guttural conk conk.

They walked away, leaving ducks and dark rock crevices, the forgotten water holding a few clouds in its smoky depths, and began to climb a hill. Squirrels ran along the ground, flickering at them, their paws crossed in brightness when they sat up to stare. As they climbed higher, past SASSAFRAS TREE, AMERICAN LINDEN TREE, the sun enclosed them in widening levels of light. Several pigeons veered, a slate V, over a pagoda and pointed, like deploying planes, to the city's wall of buildings to the west. She was climbing into air, into the weightless atmosphere the pigeons took so easily in their wings. Before them at the hill's summit was a gray stone tower, with weather vanes, revolving balls, and an American flag at the top. They made their way to it and came out on a broad platform with a wall, a drop of cliff. To the north was a large area of ground ugly with piles of broken stones and a black excavator holding steel-crossed arms in Sunday silence. "There used to be a reservoir there," John said. She turned then to the west where a strong wind was bending a group of trees. In a moment its force reached her and she breathed deeply with an involuntary spasm. The breath was all of summer; after it was fear.

30

THE FOLLOWING day she missed the usual sound of children from the street—the volume was curiously diminished—and when she went out, she saw that there were only the younger children playing. The older boys who, in play or not, organized the life of the street were gone; the older girls too were gone. The smaller children looked forsaken; their strength, their knowledge of living in their own world was not the same.

Towards the middle of the afternoon the street noise changed and the usual sound returned. She went out and walked up and down; the sidewalks were filled, shouts of the continual desperate life sounded among the buildings, was swollen in the doorways. Out of the now usual crowds of children she saw Mary leaning against a railing looking, compassionately, at a child just beginning to walk. She made her way to her and said hello.

"Hello. I saw you last night," Mary said. "That was your husband, wasn't it?"

Coming home from the park. "Yes."

"He's nice."

The little child Mary had been watching fell down and began to cry. Mary went and picked it up, holding it sidewise on her hip, balancing her body against it. The child stopped crying and looked around, happy at being held.

"I went to school today," Mary said.

The words she had expected.

"Yes?"

"Yes, the first day."

From Mary bent affectionately over the smaller child came the announcement that had been pressing at her lips, at the lips of her mind: that summer had ended. It was as warm, the sun was as full as before, but with this admission, its light changed. She turned and looked. Light on the upper parts of buildings, flaming out across the street from shafts of alleys, building gaps, dropping downward over the lower buildings with its heat. And yet it was wounded, these children had wounded it, and from now on it must slowly weaken, not to die, but to retreat, slowly to draw away and lose itself.

Go back to the room. A refuge. The room would not change; it was without seasons, nothing lived in it except the enduring shape of its walls, the routine of what must day by day be done in it. Darkness. She accepted its darkness; she went into the kitchen and turned on the light—this hard light had no change at all. Work, hide herself in the room.

She had some clothes drying on the roof; she decided to leave them until John came home. When he came, she said there were some clothes she had forgotten on the roof, and asked him if he would like to go up with her to get them. They went up together and he helped her take the clothes down, piling them in her arms. The clothes had no warmth in them now, but were dry and strangely cool. She stood with him for a minute, the wash stiff in her arms, looking out over the city, the sprawling roofs, to the city's horizon. In the after-light of sun solidifying behind the buildings, she saw a few lines of smoke above a few chimneys. She had seen them before, and yet it was now different; it reminded her of the fires of fall. She shivered. The roof on which she stood became liquid, a river. The days that she had lived in the house poured against her, a torrent, washing away, vanishing. She turned and went quickly to the door at the stairhead and climbed down into the darkness and silence of the building.

3 I

DURING the next several weeks, the weather became cooler. There was a feeling of early fall in the air; on cloudy or rainy days particularly she noticed at last a rawness that made the streets bleak. The clouds, even over the city streets, had the look she remembered from childhood and the open country, of piling grayness, a pallor of cold light hanging under them. She looked up between the buildings and spots of light glowed under the clouds; they brought the cold close. To escape it, she kept as much as she could in the room.

She had seen Anna once or twice and often thought of her. The thought of Anna opened the world to her in spite of the cold, of what she had begun to feel as the narrowing of time. She saw another room and its windows, the odor of a different house. Mr. Tannik. They were beginning to suffer. Their condition was becoming worse; they had had a small reserve which had given out. Rowe, who had made more than Anna, had had her pay cut. She thought of them, and her own fear and the proportions of her trouble lessened. Anna, in a moment of anguish, had told her that Al was helping them, that at first she had concealed it from her mother, but had finally let her know and now all of them concealed it from her father. What Al could do, though, was little. They had still heard nothing about the job in Cleveland, and the longer they went without hearing about it, the more it grew in their minds. "Mother keeps telling Father not to count on it, that something will come along, but I can see she is beginning to think about it the same as he does."

One morning the weather turned warm; it was a return of warmth almost like that of summer. Going out, she found the sun around her, over her, reassuring in sudden heat. She felt happy and began to walk, going along streets she had not seen in a long time. When, on her way back, she passed the church a few blocks away, she saw a woman stop in the vestibule and make the sign of the cross. The sign swept up and flattened to the dome; when she turned away, wherever she looked she saw it against the sky. Cross, crucifixion—She walked on slowly and before going in the gate, walked up and down near the stable, looking at the small children in the street. Children; if she could go back. No child was crucified.

In the afternoon she went out again into the warm streets, and when she returned, lay down on the bed with some of the ease and peace of the summer. How long it had been! Day by day, long, lived, so that it was almost widened to a life. The black-smith's hammer clanged down the street; it might be her first day in the room. She remembered that day's indecision, now come to what end? End. Beginning. She turned on the bed with sweat running under her arms. It was time to get John's dinner. As she got up, she wondered if he would come early. The overtime had let up, but still intermittently, sometimes several nights a week, he had to work late—

At five thirty, as usual, he came. The warmth of the day was still in the building; the light seemed greater. The windows were open, and as he kissed her, with the door open behind him, a current of air was drawn in like a wind of summer. She felt happy. He was less tired than usual, although always the day's work, now much harder, showed in his face. They ate dinner and afterward he sat talking to her while she washed the dishes. As she thought of all the days behind them, there were tears in her eyes. Happiness. This warm day, an echo of summer, weakened her; something in her gave way.

"I spoke to Meyer today," John said. Meyer; she remembered something that had happened the week before. John had come home one night seeming quieter than usual; he had talked very little during dinner. She knew that he had something on his mind, and afterward he said, "I want to speak to you about something—"

"What?"

"You know what I've told you about the shop. It's one of the worst in the city." He went over several things: pay; "Girls, unionized in another shop, are running machines we made and getting paid more by the hour than we are"; accidents; working conditions. "What we need," he had said finally, "is a union. You take this place I was telling you about where the girls make more than we do—well, their bosses say, 'Look, you make more than the men who build the machines. Why should we pay you so much.' It's a disgrace to put up with such conditions." The men were talking union; there was one new man, Herman Meyer, in particular, who seemed to know what to do. "Meyer has had some experience. But he needs somebody who's been a long time in the shop to back him up." He paused. "He'd like me to do it."

"You should," she said.

He said he believed Meyer knew how to manage it, but there was a chance if they got found out— "What?" "Well, they'd fire us."

"And then—"

"Well, you know what it would mean—"

She said, "You want to do it, John. And if you want to do it, I want you to do it."

But he had not looked satisfied.

As she looked at him now, she realized that behind what they had said had been something they had not really admitted to each other. He had hesitated because—but her mind drew back.

She finished the dishes, and as usual when they were leaving the kitchen, he reached up for the chain of the light. For the first time in a long time she was conscious of the darkness springing up behind her. The front room was still light and warm; a peculiar warmth of light was reflected in from the buildings outside, the last from the sun. He walked over to the window. "It's a beautiful evening," he said. Then he lay down on the bed and she took the evening paper he had brought home and they both began to read. Slowly the light outside faded. They talked for a while, and getting up from the bed, John said, "Want to take a walk?"

The air was still warm. In any case, she would be with him. Lately, because of his working late and her own desire to stay indoors, they had stayed most of the time in the room. Now she said, "All right, let's go." She would see the streets again at night. Streets; she remembered the street the night she went down into the subway, the fires.

They started down the stairs, and although she was not sure, she thought she heard the gate clang. When they came out into the courtyard, Anna came into it from the opposite side. She walked quickly, not looking up or noticing them until she was almost to them. "Oh!" she said. "Oh, Harriet!" Her face, as the light burning behind the stable struck it, showed inconceivably changed. "Harriet!" she said, "I had to tell you. My father got the job!"

"He did! Oh, I'm awfully glad, Anna!" Harriet said.

"Al and I are going to get married."

Anna suddenly took her in her arms.

32

Two DAYS later, she woke up feeling restless. She got John his breakfast and made the lunch he took to work, and as always, kissed him good-by. When he had gone, her restlessness increased. She began doing the breakfast dishes, and stopped several times and walked out in the other room. The third time she did it, she stood motionless and blackness moved up her body.

She thought, It won't come for a day or two. By strength of will she went into the kitchen and went on working. Each cup slowly turned, moving in her mind. She wanted to make the bed; the covers were at her fingers. Even if she could hold her body, the darkness was rising in it. It was the end. Still time, if it had only come when he was there. To wait alone all day, the body moving and driven; she took a towel and began to dry the dishes. She was standing in the doorway with a cup. What is that sound, the paws of Rocco's dog on the stairs, it was shot. Changing, the tuc tuc tuc tuc its dark roar. Multum oblita a passage marked long ago. How long before he would come home, the long day, dropping oil, smoke—O Johnny O my honey, his teeth are almond white. Those other teeth, dried white, Demuth. Time's end. The dishes finished, she went into the other room and slowly made the bed. Love. It was there it had happened. A sheet wrinkled; she carefully pulled it smooth, yet it was away from the bedhead. Rosalie and the mother Mary where she went, the corridors. She stood up and walked to see the sun it was morning, still morning.

The day ahead, now passing; she was afraid to go to the stores. It was now that her brother began to return. She moved away from it and it moved slowly. The dam had been rotted a long time. When they walked along the base beam, water poured through the planks; they looked at their reflections in the pool. "He looked at the water in the ship's pool, in the dark, but he had an hour yet to stay on duty and when he came back afterward, he dived from a twelve foot platform not knowing the water had been let out." Yesterday she had been happy, when there was time. Lean Absolom, hair entangled in the pool. O my son my brother. Where, beyond moss? Mother, you kneeled in front of it reading the three names, stone. He was sleeping now, under them, and could tell them his love. She got up from the bed and walked a long time going from the kitchen to the bed.

If this were the last day, if never again this room. She went to the armchair where he had slept the first night, touched it. This table, chair, bed, never again; to fade and blur and end in nothingness. But the chair fell down. A burning point of blackness revolved out of terror, drowning the sun. From the street she heard the sounds of the children that now had a lower alto. A taxi somewhere prolonged its brakes against fear.

When would he come? The afternoon deepened the room's shadow and the sound of children. A hoof struck; it was Pacemaker, ferried away. Sky over sound blinded the windows; had held her in his arms, Victory. To see them work, over the machines. Where is rain, the day of fear? She thought, He will be hungry. She began early to prepare his dinner. It was long, the time to cut and pare these are his potatoes. Blue gas, the kitchen reaching with its black towards night; she stopped because afterward the meat. And if she read? b. April 14, 1906—d. July 22, 1926. Those were the letters, numbers across the glazed granite. O Absolom my son his hair my brother, death.

His dinner was warm, waiting. The flames were turned low and steam escaped from the lids it was warm she went in the front. Sitting on the table edge by the window, she was able slowly to think. He must come and I must tell him. Yet when he came, how could she tell him? How could she say, This is the end. She looked over the blackness, its width in her eyes, and got up and walked up and down. He was not coming. Work had increased lately; the last two nights. Late, overtime. The minutes caught at the dark. At the far end of the room the twilight, night, was coming. The darkness not yet seen, the exigence. It was a line, pressing against her body. Beyond, it would be different; afterward, it would be changed. A hidden river, blackness, under her feet she looked down and ran to the door John John she raised her hands up against it pressed her body to it why haven't you come?

Outside the door, in the building, in the courtyard, it was dark, silent. She went into the kitchen its bareness; pulling out a drawer in the table, she took out a knife. Death. She looked at it steadily and thought, This would finally be the end, the only peace. Never again to dream; to be quiet, not think. Thin piece of steel, that in a moment could pour out her breath; then there would be nothing. Her arm tightened and she put the point to her breast. As she began to press, she heard the gate clang.

33

HE CAME in, where she was still standing in the kitchen. "God, I'm tired," he said. The knife under her hand; she left it and went to him. He had been late three nights; she could see the fatigue accumulated and heavy in his body. Like a child. "Sit down," she said. She took off his shirt and undershirt, poured water; she wet a cloth and began to wash him, rubbing the warm water all over his front and back. She kissed his hair.

"Thank you, dear," he said. While she was drying him, he reached up his arms and kissed her.

She helped him put on a clean shirt and set him in a chair at the table. "I'm sorry the dinner won't taste so good," she said. "I've had it on the stove keeping it warm." "It's good," he said, eating. "Anything is good."

When the meal was over, he went in the front room; she could tell from that that he must be very tired. She would like to have said to him, "Stay here," but she knew that he was going to lie down. It was hard for her to do the work; her restlessness increased, and several times she went to the door.

When she had finished she turned the light out and entered the front room. He was lying on the bed, his arms out wide and his breast flat and tired under the clean white shirt she had put on him. The world within her was somehow different, with him here. Darkness the same, and yet her sight steadied by him. There was the slow sound of an auto passing in the street; she heard under it the sound of a child pulling a wagon. She must tell him now, she thought; she stood looking at him. How could she tell him? She must; if she did not, it— If she did not, he would see her. He must not see. She took a step towards him, the words had almost begun when she thought, One last night. Just this night. I can tell him in the morning. To have him, in peace through one more night. To be with him in love, for the last night.

She lay down quietly on the bed beside him and he put his arm around her. "It's good just to lie this way," he said. He pressed the hair back from her forehead and kissed her. His lips lay against her; his slow breath was on her cheek. When the room darkened, he said, "Shall we go to bed?" "Yes," she said. When he was in bed, at once, with a sigh, he turned on his back and lay flat and inert. "John," she said. "What, dear?" She kissed him. He did not respond; she knew that he wanted her to let him go to sleep, she understood the overwhelming tiredness in his body, and how he needed sleep. Yet she thought, This is the last time. It will never be again. She kissed him and moved her hand gently across his body. He moved a little but immediately became still again and his breathing deepened. She could not. She could not bring herself to break his sleep, to force his tiredness. She lay quietly beside him and now, with the stillness of her body, she began to feel the motion and pitch of her mind. At its surface, unlike the still untouched center, she was unprotected. Outside were sounds, the ticking of the clock, a breeze rustling a cord or wire somewhere outside the house. As these sounds lessened, she heard a low sound of street traffic. Far away, the report of two shots; saw the rifle, the dog. He was asleep now, his breathing slow, deep, and regular. She closed her eyes. Time roaring away BWAY SEVENTH AVENUE, EXPRESS to midnight; the darkness plunged. John— To sleep, "sleep." City. The light behind the stable made a square on the ceiling; even through her closed eyes she could see it. It had no lines of bars and as she looked, hardly visible and then deepening the lines appeared, firm, dark, bars that she could see. The light was out. What? She lifted her head.

John beside her stirred. "What is it?" he said. She turned hard against his body. "I want you," she said. His body woke; she felt desire grow in him. He caught her shoulder, she turned under him. In a moment she felt herself rush to him; her legs, her whole being gripped him. Darkness, slowness. When at last he became still over her, he said, "What is it? Why are you crying?"

"I—you've made me so happy," she said.

"You mustn't cry," he said.

She herself became still and now she began to wait. But nothing. Only tiredness began to grow in her, the usual tiredness. John was lying beside her; at last he took his arm from under her body and changed his position, to go to sleep.

She went to sleep too and in the morning the restlessness had gone.

PART THREE

I

It was early April; a sudden warmth had entered the building and courtyard. She stood at the window, looking out now particularly at the light, the strong sun. The window was open and there was nothing between her and the sun; it lay warm on her skin, like the air that stirred her hair, moving its blackness back across her shoulders. It was a year since she had stood at the window in the hospital and looked out at the spring beginning there. A year. April. A year from death, and so the longest year. During half of it, she had moved towards death, but the winter just passed, what had it been? A going towards hope?

She moved back out of the sun and looked down at the table. On it, the three books, the same that had always stood there: the Bible, *The Pilgrim's Progress*, the *Machine Shop Practice*. Soon after she had come with John, she had read *The Pilgrim's Progress*; she picked it up now and turned to its last pages. "Now, when they were come up to the gate, there were written over, in letters of gold, 'Blessed are they that do his commandments, that they may have a right to the tree of life, and may enter in, through the gates, into the city.'" Into the city. She closed the book and put it, slowly, back by the other books. She thought, But when?

Leaning now on the top of the lower half of the window, she breathed the spring air. Behind her a stove, against the side wall, was out for the first time. November when John had bought it—a small round object of iron which they had fitted with a pipe into the wall. It had kept them warm all winter and she had grown to like it, feeding it coal which was darkness. Coal, darkness,

209

becoming heat. Yet she was glad now that it was out, that the faint odor of coal gas was being blown from the room. Coal, the mines. The winter, which had brought the coal into their room, brought night; at three thirty or four she had had to put on the lights and it was black night when John came home. Yet under it was that waiting that she had never known before, delay, hope? The day after the day when she had overcome her restlessness, she had told John about it. She had said, "It never happened before." John wanted to think of her, particularly as time went on and no restlessness recurred, as well—"cured." She could not agree with him, she knew that she was not yet well. The change, the hope, was that now she might some day know what would at last make her well.

The spring air was warm and yet had in it still the feeling, as in the country, that it had come over melting snow. A last coldness, not fear, only freshening in the currents of the wind. This light against her. Sun, which in the fall had been withdrawing, was now strengthening, rising, a resurrection over the warming city. There were no birds coming back, only the ever-present sparrows; no trees that could be seen from the windows; but it was spring, life and birth again. In the sounds, the noise of the children, of the street traffic, the city's perpetual sound, were subtle sounds of the season. It was something new, changed; it was the air of spring.

She heard a faint angry barking upstairs and trembled. Echo. But was it an echo, or did all things return? Not long ago, as though the coming of spring had made a change in Rocco's heart, he had brought home with him another dog, as defiant as the one that had been killed. "I find him," he said to John. "You don't mind I have a dog again? Not bark much—" One night, when everything had been quiet, they had heard a crash on the stairway. There had been apparently a little difficulty; they heard Rocco yelling at the dog in Italian, but soon there was a familiar patter on the stairs. "He's bringing back the meatbone," John said.

Breathing the air deeply, she looked down at the courtyard. Hardly changed, a little dirtier from melted snow, the tinge of winter. Frost had made new cracks in the cement, in the so-called paving. Yet the evidences of winter were small, only to be seen, like the signs of spring, by the heart that feels small changes. The room too had its changes from winter, but because of her need of its permanence they too were small, only what had been absolutely necessary. The stove; extra covers on the bed, soon to come off; the coal scuttle. Besides these, several hard new chairs, put in inconspicuous corners, which were brought out when some men from the shop came to talk with John and Herman Meyer. Meyer and some of the other men who were taking a lead in organizing the union were coming for a meeting tonight. She turned her back to the window and thought, The room needs cleaning. The city so quickly sifted its dirt, its grit, inside, laying a layer of discoloration on the woodwork, on everything. The floor should be scrubbed; she liked the clean look of the floor boards after she had washed them. How many times? Repetition. Yet she would not clean it today. Today was too tender; the unsettling atmosphere required a different answer from work.

She turned again to the window and for some reason thought of her mother. She had thought of her once before. It had been an evening about two months ago when John had been worried—a bench hand at the shop, Joe Miller, had proved to him that another man he was depending on was a "rat." Later the thought of her mother had come. A moment of pity had surged up in her, as it had at their visit to the hospital, and she said, "I'd like to write my mother and father that I'm well. I don't want to take the chance, though, of letting them know where I am." John had said, "I know what to do. We'll send a letter to Jimmy, to mail from Ohio." She had written the letter and he had sent it to his brother. Her mind had closed afterward; she felt no nearer to them than before. Why?

And now her thoughts turned to her brother. In a few days it would be his birthday. All morning she realized she had been trying not to think of him. Was he death? It could not be that. She paused for a moment. From across time, like a voice somewhere heard: "Brethren, be not children in understanding" Where? "but in understanding be men." Again: "So when this corruptible shall have put on incorruption, and this mortal shall have put on immortality, then shall be brought to pass the saying that is written, Death is swallowed up in victory."

Where? There was something she did not know. If she knew? She could relinquish him, let the shadow of him out of her. The room was warm. The cracked white ceiling seemed to tremble with the spring air running under it. A faint sound came from the street...

A week ago she and John had gone one evening to visit Anna, who lived now with Al on Columbus Avenue near the building where she had lived before with her parents. They had gone early, before dark. As they left the El, she said, "Let's walk up around the park again." They went up 110th and turned up the avenue below the Cathedral. She remembered the first time they had walked there, the color of that night. No darkness now, only the first yellowing twilight in the sky. Trees came above the railing beside them; she could see the start of leaves, life ready to be thrown over the bare park.

That evening, in confidence, Anna had told her she was going to have a baby. "I'm awfully glad," she said. Anna said jokingly, "Now it's your turn. Now you have no excuse—" "That's right," she said, not letting her voice change. She wondered immediately how she was going to tell John. A week had gone by and she had not yet been able to tell him. Spring; it burned in her. Birth. "The last enemy that shall be destroyed is death." Life had not died with him; it could not be killed. Only she had died. But had she?

She went into the kitchen to eat. This midday meal, the only one she ate alone, still after almost a year, oppressed her. The light of the one bulb shone hard, flat, and changeless. A heart of night, beating. It hardly seemed that the spring day could come in here, the whisper of it was lost at the kitchen door. For a moment she thought it was winter, and that the warmth came not from spring but from the belly of the stove. Winter. One morning in midwinter she had woken up after John had left and had looked at the windows, covered with frost. Palms, ferns of frost. She had stared. Covered with silence. Through curves of the frost, icy leaves, was a vague shape, flat brick walls, webbed porches—She had run to the window and pressing her hand to it, had melted it.

As soon as she finished eating, she went again into the front room, into its light and warmth. Sun, in air that came unobstructed through the open upper halves of the two windows. It was not cold. Warm. The light, the sky was growing with spring. She felt a desire to go out, into the streets. She went and put on her jacket, the same she had worn from the hospital and had put away in the fall when the weather became too cold. She closed and locked the room door behind her, and went downstairs, feeling unaccustomed air from the open house door below. She crossed the courtyard, smelling of thaw, and went out into the street. All at once she was in the midst of the clamor of children, the younger ones because the others were still in school. The sound was free, she could feel it; their shouts had no longer a roof of cold over them. During the winter the children had been pushed back into the houses; now the doors that had been closed all winter were opening, the children were coming out, were taking possession of the street. Bare skin under sweaters, soon the young bodies would be freed and given to summer.

The street looked clean in a contrast to winter, when, except in the few hours just following a snowfall, it had been black, mottled, garbage and snow a solid mass, layer by layer. Ashes of bonfires, urine. Now after the thawing of spring, janitors got out hoses and flushed down the walks in front of their buildings, scouring away every mark. The street was wet, cold, and clean; in a few weeks it would dry into summer. She looked with new eyes at the buildings. A laundry door was open; she looked through it at vats spilling water and steam. A curve of hot soapy water swirled out the door, across the sidewalk. Soap, astringent health.

In the city and in the country was the cleansing of spring. The odor of beginning, of birth, of liquid torrents penetrating, cleaning and preparing for birth. She walked slowly and came to the pushcarts. In winter they had been cold, dulled like the weather. Now they were cleansed and freshened; water no longer froze and they were sprinkled again with the watering cans. She looked up at the sky. It was clean, a cloud was forming behind the church; the church was flat, cold, as she had always known it, but the cross, like a separate thing, was not cold but fiery. Cross, crucifixion. Death. "The last enemy that shall be destroyed is death."

She did some shopping and started back. Again the street, children. Quiet now, but soon school would be out and the older children would come, filling the street with a fuller sound. A new breath was in their lungs, new looseness and strength in their movements. They seldom looked away from each other, but when they did look, by accident, into the eyes of a "*uomo*," their gaze appeared hard and hostile. Enemies, youth and "them." Of all the children, Mary was the only one to whom she talked or to whom the fact of man appeared to exist. She thought it must be because Mary cared for the younger children; her eyes had compassion. Lately she had talked with her more often; the world of the many families living in the street was opening to her. Such a woman was the "grandmother" of such a child. Somebody came to see Joe Vinogrado's father after he didn't do "his job." "What job?" "I don't know," Mary said. "That's Vittorio." The most important news Mary had had in a long time was that she could now talk to Rosalie. "But she's still married." "What happened?" "Father Crocitto forgave her. And 'he' still doesn't believe in heaven." As she walked along the street now, she thought of Mary and wished she were here.

The gate. Bleached by winter, the lozenges of its overlapping metal bands concealed the shadow of the passageway. Gate to home, home? How many times she had opened and closed it— listened, waiting for John in the evening, for its warning clang. It clanged now and the sound was followed almost immediately by the restive movement of a horse inside the stable in some stall on the second floor. Stable. City? A faint odor of manure—stable, screaming, "Father! Father!" She went slowly on, crossed the courtyard, and climbed the stairs to the room. Softness of spring, of air that even now was blowing in the room; it came through the open windows and escaped in the cracks around the hallway door. She took off her jacket and stood for a long time in this current of the air, that touched her hair, her face and crept among the folds of her dress. Window, the sun had gone. Yet she could still see it, hot in the air, drying the last damp of winter from the stable, from other buildings. When she felt almost drunk with sun, with so much air, she went into the kitchen where in silence and artificial night, she began to prepare dinner. Always when she began to get dinner ready, she thought of John. She could see him plainly, at his machine; she had been to the shop and now had the image, the sound of it in her. Knowledge; nobody can tell you, she thought.

One morning in late fall, before the first snow, he had agreed to take her with him to work. They had gone out into the streets together, which were cold, with long shadows—the sun could hardly be seen behind the buildings. At this hour even the subway was different; now there were few or almost no women, only men, laborers. When they came out, she saw reddish brick walls, stained and blackened by smoke, a territory of three or four story buildings. Flat walls; warehouses, factories. As they started down a block of warehouses, a truck backed to the curb ahead of them and when it stopped, several men began to unload bundles of paper from it. They worked fast, some of them putting the bundles on the sidewalk in disorder while others took them into a small building entrance. Watching the men unloading the truck were several groups of idle men, standing on the curb or in nearby doorways. Their faces were hard; as Harriet and John walked past, one of them said loudly, "How do they like their jobs, the scabs."

Two blocks further on they came to the shop, a building silent in the morning light. She looked up at dirty windows and the whole interior of the building seemed dead. "In here," John said, and they went in a door. Hallway. She began to hear the hum of machines, the breath of belts. Going through a small office, John opened a door and said, "Go inside and look around; I'll be with you in a minute." She went into the shop, hesitant, alone in an unfamiliar world. The entire floor of the shop, a fairly large area, was covered with machines, of different shapes and sizes. Men were already standing at them, beginning work. She stood between a machine marked LEBLOND NO 11/2 HEAVY DUTY and a workbench; she watched a man at work. He lifted a tin can of a milky fluid into a receptacle over the Leblond machine. She watched him pour it in, put down the can, and brush what looked like a small piece of pipe with a small paint brush. It was this piece of pipe that was to be, what? he moved his arm, a grinder pressed down, and a long tube began to let the "soap water" fall on the point of contact. A faint steam curled up. John was standing beside her. "How do you like it?" he said. She could say nothing. Belts made a flapping sound. Click of wheels, gears; then a whine or sharp whir in the larger sound. Clank of presses. Light came down through half-open skylights and blazed from a row of windows at the far side of the room. "Is your lathe here?" she said. "Yes. Do you want to see it?" "Yes." Yet as he started along a half-defined aisle among the machines, she stopped. "No, I'm afraid," she said. "You go on alone." He went on and she returned to her place near the door, to safety. There she watched him reach his machine and begin work, his head and shoulders dark against the solid eastern light of the windows.

Since then it had been easier to be alone all day, because she knew where he was and could see him, in her mind, at work. She thought of him most often, as now, towards late afternoon, the end of the day when he would be coming home. Now too he would be thinking of her, of what she was doing. Between them, the place where he was and the place where she was, there was now no separation.

She had the dinner cooking, with flames turned low, and went into the other room. While she had been in the kitchen, it had changed. Walls darker. The ceiling a little more vague, gathering under it with the current of spring air the first shadows of night. The midday was longer now, and the peculiar afternoon twilight that had always begun so early in the room was at least later now than it had been during the winter, when the room had seemed to darken as soon as the morning sun left it. But now the night was already in it, growing downward. It would not be quite night by the time John came, but when the men came for the union meeting, it would be entirely dark. Light. Circle under the light. She thought of the men, the circle repeated, changed, yet always the same, the faces of the shop. Meyer. The bench hand, Joe Miller, whom John liked. Others; Vogel, a grinder; Schwartz, Meyer's helper; Hollering; Kramer, who worked on a milling machine; a sweeper, Johnson. She was not part of this circle, she even kept physically outside of it. Yet she liked to look at them, to hear them, to hear the conversation, no matter what it might be. What they spoke of was often technical, "shop talk"; not understanding it reminded her of times when she could not understand what was said when she was a child. Now, though, while she might not get the details, she understood the general meaning of what was said. Much too that was not said. Faces were a speech. Meyer's face in particular she liked to look at—square, German, soft only at the lips. She remembered one night when Hollering, a die maker and an influential man whom Meyer wanted to keep in the union, had been arguing with Meyer on a point that came up. Meyer had bluntly said, "I tell you the union has god to have sweepers, has god to have every bracked of workers. Otherwise nothing. If you tool and die makers—" he was angry—"think you can ged anywhere alone, you're making a big mistake. You can only raise yourself by raising the resd along with you." Hollering "took" it. Words poured and echoed in her, yet they did not seem important to her. What was important was the faces that were in front of her; Meyer's face always leaning forward, aggressive. His lips were not weak, only soft at the edges. Vogel was almost always resting with his head back; he said little, always listened. Faces and voices; John and Meyer, working together, almost in this slowly growing work a single entity.

She heard a low hiss of steam coming from the kitchen, and went to see that the cooking was going all right. John would come any minute now. When she had added a little water to one pot, she went to the window and sat watching the courtyard. The other window, bars. There had been trees outside of it. But this was more beautiful; only the cement worn by winter, the bare walls. Once in the recent January there had been rain and she had thought of spring. Now it was here. Two weeks ago it had rained for the first time: a persistent gray and even sound that was the spring itself. Revealing again the surface of the courtyard, giving it its wetness. As she sat thinking of it, the gate clanged.

Driven by an impulse, the same that had made her go out into the sun in the afternoon, she ran from the room and down the stairs. At the lower house door she saw him coming; he was framed against the outside light, the air of spring. Machines, Victory. She ran and threw herself against him, held him. "Dear, how good it is to see you!" she said. "I've been waiting for you all day." He kissed her and they climbed the stairs together, awkwardly trying to do it with their arms around each other. At the landing, he himself opened the door.

Smell of cooking, twilight in the room. "It's warm, isn't it?" she said.

"Yes, it was warm in the shop. It's spring, all right."

"It is spring. I haven't felt it before the way I felt it today. I was happy all day, and I've been thinking."

"Of what?"

"Nothing."

"Good—" He grasped her in his arms. As he held her, she thrust her hands inside his shirt and flattened them against his breast. They stood still; in silence they pressed towards each other—she listened. Crucifixion. "But some man will say, How

are the dead raised up?" Fainter "Thou fool, that which thou sowest is not quickened, except it die." Where? The room returned
out of her pulse; all the strangeness and freedom of spring in it
and in the air flowing against the ceiling. Open window, the sun
upon the earth, sky, acute in the hour before night. She let her
hands fall and John lifted her head and kissed her along the tem-
ple. "You are so beautiful," he said.

"What time are they coming?" she asked.

"I asked Meyer to come a little early. He'll be here soon."

"Then we'd better hurry. Why didn't you bring him for dinner?"

"He couldn't come." As they were eating, he said, "You know,
Meyer likes you."

"Yes," she said, "he does. He's good, isn't he."

They talked, as they often did, of the men in the shop. "Joe
Miller tells me his sister is coming down to see him from Boston.
He's going to show her the town." Sister. "He showed me her
photograph." Brother, Joe's sister had her brother.

"Was she nice?"

"Yes."

Alive, could walk the streets together, talk—

"I guess it's the spring," she said. "But let it be spring." Birth.
Foreverlasting advent.

Meyer came while she was washing the dishes. She went to the
kitchen door and said hello, and John stayed in the front room
and they began to talk. She could hear their voices come into the
kitchen; everything contracted into their voices; work, walls, the
bark of Rocco's dog above the ceiling. It was John's voice she listened for. Known, loved syllables. The earth sank beyond them
into night.

When she was finished, she went in the front room. "Sit still,"
she said as Meyer got up. They had lit the light. "I don't know
what it is about this room, it gets dark so early," she said. "The
ceiling iss low," Meyer said, "and id's a deep room." "Maybe that's
it." "Also id looks east." As she drew her chair to face them, Meyer

said, "I saw your *Madonna an der Treppe* as I wass coming in."
"*Madonna an der Treppe*" was his nickname for Mary; it meant,
he had said, the madonna of the staircase. She had told him about
Mary one evening. "I was hoping I might see her this afternoon,
but I didn't," she said. "I can see how you like her," he said. "She
has such beautiful eyes, eyes as you say of a madonna." In every
man, she thought, there's softness. Meyer's lips; if he were in love,
his lips would be beautiful. John—In John it was the memory of
the mines—a scar, a little blue of coal dust, below his left breast-
point. Darkness in his flesh.

She forgot, as they talked, all thought, all going backward or
forward. Twilight had really fallen now over the earth; the air,
turning dark, still kept its warmth and buoyancy. When it was
quite dark, the gate clanged and three men came together across
the courtyard. She recognized Hollering, although it was hard to
see. The men came up the stairs, they made a loud sound in the
house; John opened the door for them and brought them in. The
two other men who came with Hollering were Kramer and
Schwartz, Meyer's helper. The group as usual made a rough circle
as if pivoted outward from the light which hung in the center of
the room. The night outside the windows was a flat darkness; the
air that came in held the smell of spring. She took a seat at the
edge of the circle, not really a part of it and yet not outside.

Getting awkwardly to business, without formality, the men
began to discuss some of the pressing problems of the union. She
thought, as she often had before, how much talk was necessary
for a little action, how slowly they advanced; it was hard sometimes to feel even that anything had been accomplished. Yet perhaps more was accomplished than appeared; she knew that the
union was becoming stronger, was slowly growing. When, after
long argument, the specific "business" of the meeting was finished and general talk began, a certain shop was mentioned.
"What was that?" John said. "To go back," Meyer said. "Four
yearss ago, one of the worsd shops in New York stade was run, up
in a little town—Linville I think id wass, upstade. They orga-

nized a very strong union and pulled a strike. The guy who owned thiss shop tried to break id. They stayed oud four months. 'All righd,' thiss guy said, 'I'll move oud of town.' And he did. He moved his business to a differend town, a hundred miless away, more than a hundred. Bud the union followed him. Now he'ss god another strike, differend people bud he couldn'd escape." The men listened attentively. "He deserves to get put out of business." She had often noticed the interest of the men in other shops, cities. They knew names and places, names of owners, bosses, they understood policies, knew different methods of paying wages, knew whether shops had a good or bad reputation for accidents, knew particularly the union development of the shops. "Such and such a shop is all union." Or, "The union scale at such and such a shop is so much."

The conversation became less interesting. Hollering insisted on describing in detail a development in the manufacture of a "part" vital to electrical refrigerators. He kept repeating, "Two ten-thousandths of an inch." Unfortunately, she thought, Kramer was interested and Meyer, who had in mind Hollering's influence in the shop, was showing an interest too. She slowly forgot what was being said, began to look idly in front of her, across her foot, at the coal scuttle. There was a bright worn spot in the center of the handle, where her hand all winter had held it; John's hand too. At the base was another place where their hands had touched, tipping the coal into the fire. Winter, fire. The stove was dead, another warmth had supplanted it. The interior life was supplanted by an outside one, by the air still coming in with the freshness of spring. "Life—" The worn metal, the spot polished by their two hands. Coal, darkness. "Darkness." The men's voices rose and fell, she heard nothing. "The last enemy that shall be destroyed is death." Where? "Thou fool, that which thou sowest—" The metal glowed; all at once she knew. It was the burial service, the words said over her brother's grave. And over all graves, the words of death and resurrection.

"Well, there's work tomorrow," Meyer said. The men were

getting up, preparing to leave. She and John said good night to them, holding out their hands. "Thank you for being so patiend," Meyer said. "I don'd know how you do id." "Sometimes I forget you," she said. "Yah. Tonight id wass in your face, you were nod with us, you were yourself a *Madonna an der Treppe*." Meyer followed the other men out and John left the door open while they started down the dark well of the stairs. "All right?" he said. "Yes. Yes." The voices receded; she could hear the steps from floor to floor, then the building was empty. John closed the door.

"John," she said. The silence that fell around them, even with the never-ceasing presence of the city, was complete. Faces, words, the look of the men was dissipated in this silence in which he and she were alone. It was as it should be. She put her arms around him and kissed him.

"I love you, dear," he said.

"I love you."

They walked to one of the open windows and looked out. "All winter we haven't looked out at the night," she said. "Do you know it?" Outside the darkness was deep, pure, reaching upward. The slightly cloudy sky was like a reflection of the courtyard; the air smelled of clouds and of the stable. Always the continuing warmth, the presence of spring. "Do you smell spring?" she said.

"Yes, I smell it."

Fence, revolving shadow of the palings; the gate.

"It's almost a year," she said.

"Yes."

In a few days it would be her brother's birthday. Anna. "I was thinking of Anna today," she said.

"Yes?"

"She told me something, that—"

He waited.

"Do I have to tell you?"

"Yes."

"She's going to have a baby."

She had known it would hurt him; it did. Al and Anna's marriage. "If any of you know any impediment why you may not lawfully join in matrimony, you may now confess it..." rapid voice, Al and Anna standing together. "...will you love, comfort, honor, and keep her as a faithful husband is bound to do—" nodding "—health and sickness, in prosperity and adversity, forsaking all others?" The replies "Yes. Yes." "I then pronounce you man and wife until death do you part."

The day Anna and Al had been married, John had asked her again to marry him.

She had said, "I'm not sure yet; dear, I can't."

"But I love you."

"It wouldn't be right. Oh, I'm not sure. Please don't try to make me, John."

He had said nothing more and it was hard to remind him of it. He was now waiting, like her. The darkness closed out of his eyes and he looked at her steadily. "I'm glad for them," he said. He bent forward and they leaned together, with their heads touching, out into the dark and the night air. If— A horse stirred in the stable. If— She heard: "It isn't a matter of belief now, just listen."

2

THREE days before her brother's birthday, something happened. When she went downstairs, as she usually did, at noon, she looked on the lower hallway table for mail for John and saw a letter to him. When she examined it, she saw that it was postmarked from the town where Jimmy lived, but was not in Jimmy's handwriting. Immediately she had a premonition of danger—had something happened to Jimmy? As long as she could remember, nobody except him had written from Ohio. She had an impulse to open the letter, but decided to wait for John.

When John came, she immediately gave him the letter and when he had read it, he handed it to her.

DEAR JOHN,

I have never ritten to you befor and I hope you will not let Jim no I am riting to you I guess you no the mine he is working in is a bad one I guess you no he is robbing pillers it is to dangerus he says he has to make mony but I wd rather starve, even have the children starve

Can you rite to him?

Your sister-in-marrage,

HANNAH

The note was written on a piece of the same paper Jim usually used, from a cheap ruled pad. She could see his wife getting out the pad, hesitating a long time before deciding to write without her husband's knowledge.

John said, "It must be pretty bad for Hannah to write that way. Probably they're getting near the bottom and expect a cave-in any day…" He broke off and said, "I'd better write right away. He's got to stop, get out of there. I suppose they're in debt—I'll tell him God damn it not to be a fool and let me know how much he needs. I'll—" He stopped and getting paper, began to write the letter. His hand moved quickly; he bore down, though, as if to make heavier, more forceful, the words that were to influence his brother. "Meyer will let me have some money; we'll get some money somehow." As he wrote, she knew what he was thinking. He knew the mines; the mines were now in his mind's eye, the sound, the odor were recalled—all the deaths he had seen. Darkness opening—

When he finished the letter, he said, "I'll mail it now. I'll be right back." While he was gone, she thought of Jimmy. Why did men take such chances, why did they keep on, why didn't they stop? And the more terrible question, who let them do it? Who gave them money to make them risk their lives?

When John came back, he was preoccupied and silent. They sat together looking at the darkness which was beginning to clot over the roofs. He's thinking of his brother, she thought, and did not break his silence. At last he said, "I'd give a lot to have Jim out of the mines. It's got hold of him in the wrong way." After a moment, he said, "I think he'll listen to reason. Hannah will make him." Still brooding, he got up and walked about the room. "I don't know what it is about Jimmy," he said, "that he means so damned much to me. It isn't just that he's my brother. I've always been this way. I watched out for him when I was a kid. I was pretty strong as a kid of fourteen, fifteen. Jimmy wasn't; he was sickly. I remember the year before we left home together, Jimmy was working for a man after school. One day when Jimmy was sick, the man refused to let him go home. When he did get home, he looked like a sheet. I asked him what was the trouble. He told me. 'Listen,' I said, 'you don't need that job and maybe you won't have it much longer.' I went around to the man's office and said,

'You know my brother isn't strong. When he's sick, I want you to let him go home.' The man argued about it, and I threw him down a flight of stairs."

Gradually, as night fell, John's mood changed. He became calmer and she could feel him turning to her. He needed her nearness as a woman. The silence of the night had its quieting influence too; it was a dark night without stars. She went to the window. Warmness, darkness filled with peace. Night over all the city, over Anna and Al and their baby—the child unborn. She had already seen the slight fullness of Anna's belly, the beginning of its hardness. Birth. And she thought suddenly of her brother's birth.

In three days it would be his birthday. In the past, the approach of his birthday had been filled with pain for her—he was so much the memory of his death. Yet this year she felt a change; recalling him no longer was so hard, no longer made her feel pain or bitterness. Did it mean as John said that she was well now? But she knew it was not that; unwilling as she was to admit it, she knew it was not that.

The morning of her brother's birthday, she woke up early, before John, and lay looking at the early morning sunlight coming in the room; it touched the room with pale rays hardly strong enough for shadow. She looked all around her. Chairs, table, bureau, windows. She thought of the hospital room, in which she had awakened a year ago—far as it was from her, she could see it clearly too. The window there; she remembered how she had stood in front of its bars, looking outward. Brother, if it were not for your death— It was still true; the words still true—she had not yet gone past his death. She listened to the morning air whisper along the ceiling; the sun hardened its light above her. When would she know?

John had breakfast with her and got ready to go to work as he would on any other morning. She had not told him it was her brother's birthday; after the first time she had described her brother's death and told him what it meant, she had rarely spoken of her brother. He noticed no difference from any other day.

When he had kissed her good-by, she watched for him to cross the courtyard as she always did, and he disappeared into the passageway to the street. The courtyard filled with sun. Hard hot sun lying on the seams of the concrete paving, on the clapboards of the stable. When she turned back to the room, it seemed dark.

On her brother's birthday, when he had been alive, they had always had a party. Friends, relatives had come, but in her memory she saw only him, his tall straight figure, his face across the candles on the cake. "Blow them out," he always said to her and she seemed to smell the smoke of the extinguished candles and feel her breath going to him. Brother— Too late. "Be not children in understanding" Steps sounded in the building and Rocco's dog barked. Her thought was broken; she heard the sound of the city, faint cries, the murmur of traffic. She went to the kitchen, and began her morning's work.

At twelve, out of habit, she went downstairs. As she started down, she wondered if it might be possible that there was a letter from Jimmy. Immediately after thinking of it, she felt sure there would be, yet it was a shock when looking on the table, she actually found the letter. She thought, He must be going to leave the mine. Otherwise, she was sure, he would not have answered so quickly. She carried the letter carefully upstairs and put it on the bureau; several times she came back and looked at it, at Jimmy's familiar handwriting. How happy John would be! The day now seemed to go by slowly; for John's sake she wished it would hasten. When the room darkened and she had the supper ready waiting on the stove, she went to the window to wait for him—her excitement was mounting. Rocco came in and she waved to him. Five minutes later John came.

The moment she heard his steps in the passageway, she ran down the stairs to meet him.

"There's a letter from Jimmy!" she said.

He was as excited as she was and hurried up the stairs. "Where is it!" he said. She showed him; he opened it and they read it together:

DEAR JOHN,

Ive been thinking over your letter and as you probably guess, Hannah has been working on me—so maybe your right. I dont want to die I know. If your willing to send what I need —that is, if you can—I'll quit the job and get out. Itll take eighty dollars and if you can scrape up a hundred, I could use that. But dont if you cant make it, for Im set to hang on.

Yrs

JIM

When they finished the letter, John said, "Thank God! I'll get the money for him if I have to borrow from everybody I know. They know I don't usually borrow; they know I'll pay it back." He paused. "Anyway, I'm sure Meyer will help out with a good part of it."

As they sat down to supper, she looked at him under the hard raying light of the bulb in the kitchen and thought of how he had looked that evening after the first day she had spent alone in his room. It had been different from the way he looked now; the first meeting had had about it a cast of strangeness. With time it had changed; he had become familiar and other faces than the first one had become known and loved. Familiar oval of his face, the broad sloping shoulders—her hand went out to him. "What is it?" he said.

"Nothing."

After supper, they went into the front room. They sat down and as usual, read the evening paper; the darkness slowly fell. A radio in another building announced a jazz piece and an orchestra began to play; a faint repetition in the rhythm made her think of Miss Cummings. A horse stamping in the stable. For some reason, a hardness of the horse's stamping, she thought of Miss Batras; Miss Batras had been a patient with her in the manic ward who had thought she could communicate with her relatives by pounding on her bed. The pounding and Miss Batras' emaciated appearance combined to produce a terrible impression on her; she was constantly in deadly fear of her. The thought of Miss Batras recalled to her again the horror of the manic ward, its nauseating bland odor, the sounds, the whispers. But they no longer had any power over her; at will she could forget them and feel only the peace that was around her now. She turned to John. "Dear," she said.

"What—?"

"I'd like to tell you something." She paused. "Today is my brother's birthday."

He looked up in surprise.

"I didn't tell you before. But now I want to."

"Thank you, dearest."

She said nothing more and, as always, he respected her silence. The spring air whispered above them; the darkness became deeper. They no longer were reading the paper, but only sat together in the room and were aware of the growing night. At last John said, "I think I'll go around and ask Meyer about that money. Would you like to come?"

"Yes," she said.

At that moment, a voice called in the lower part of the house. "Kohler! Anybody by the name of Kohler live here?" It came from the bottom of the stairwell; John opened the door and they heard it more clearly. "Kohler! Anybody named Kohler live here?"

John called down, "I'm Kohler. Come up here!"

A telegraph messenger, a boy, ran up the stairs and held out a telegram. "Sign, please," he said. When John had signed, the boy ran back down the stairs.

John tore open the telegram and after a moment gave it to her.

JIM KILLED TODAY IN MINE WHAT SHALL I DO
HANNAH

"Jim," he said. As he stepped back into the room, his foot caught on the coal scuttle; a few pieces of coal spilled out on the floor. His eyes filled with horror and he stumbled to a chair by the window and sank onto it.

"My brother," he said.

She listened. Death—a train rose in front of her, there was a screech of brakes and she saw her brother's body lifted, thrown through the air. Then coal: "The timbers would be crushed like matchsticks." She held to a chair. Through faintness she heard a sound; it was John crying. Sound of awkward crying; he was unused to giving expression to grief. The faintness slowly left her and she remembered.

Once when she had been a child, she had seen her father cry. She had heard the sound first and had gone to the door of his bedroom; he had been lying on the bed crying and her mother had been comforting him—she felt ashamed to see him. Yet as she looked, she recognized something: that her mother loved him. Love. Could it then be this? Why in so many years had she never remembered? It was so clear now. She could see the shadows of the bedroom, the blue squares on the quilt of the bed—she was looking into the room again as though she were again a child.

She was listening to the sound of a man crying, but it was not her father, but John. She looked. He sat bent forward, his head dark against the window; she felt need stir in her and slowly went to him and kneeling down, put her arms around him.

"John dear," she said. "I'm sorry, I'm so sorry."

Her death was ended. Now she held her arms closer around him; he put his head against hers. His tears were hot on her and as she comforted him, she thought, Now I can tell him that I know.

AFTERWORD

SEVERAL years ago, while browsing in a used bookstore, I came across a copy of *The Outward Room* by Millen Brand. In addition to its intriguing title and oddly named author, what prompted me to pick up the book was its unusual type-only jacket cover,* which prominently displayed, in three bands across the bottom third of the book, quotations from Theodore Dreiser, Sinclair Lewis, and Fannie Hurst, each heralding the book in extraordinary terms. Lewis called it a "great love story—a real love story. I don't know that I have ever seen a more exciting first novel." Hurst wrote, "*The Outward Room* is original and fascinating...The book roams into the most intricate and obscure recesses of human experiences; does it brilliantly and emerges into the sunlight." And Dreiser: "A fine book. It is one of those firmly painted, exquisite miniatures of life, rare among modern books, that contrive to be unsparing and honest, and at the same time refreshing and lovely."

The language of prepublication adulation has become so predictably and narrowly codified, but the words in those blurbs—great, exciting, original, fascinating, brilliant, fine, exquisite, unsparing, honest, refreshing, and lovely—still meant something in 1937, especially when one considers that they described a first book by an unknown writer. (About the author, Lewis wrote "to Millen Brand, of whom I know nothing whatsoever, I present my most earnest greetings.")

---

*The simultaneous edition had a conventional illustrated jacket.

I wondered how it was that I had never heard of this book and its extraordinarily promising young author. I asked around, but no one seemed to know or remember Millen Brand, or his books. It's somewhat frightening to learn that good books—even books heralded in their time—can disappear so quickly and completely. We like to think that things of enduring quality and worth are separated from the dross and permanently enshrined, but we know that this is not true. Beautiful things are more likely to disappear than to endure. *The Outward Room* is such a beautiful thing. And like so many literary treasures, much of its beauty is a result of its singularity, its ability to be both so unlike other books and yet so true to itself.

Millen Brand was born in New Jersey, in 1906, the son of a Jersey City fisherman, and graduated from the Columbia School of Journalism. Throughout most of the 1930s, he worked as an advertising copywriter for the telephone company. He arrived at the office at seven o'clock every morning, and wrote for the two hours before the start of the workday. In 1934 a story of his published in the magazine *Trend* was read by Clifton Fadiman, then an editor at Simon and Schuster. Fadiman wrote the author an encouraging and inquiring note; Brand replied that he was working on a novel; Fadiman asked to see it when it was finished. Two years later, Brand personally delivered his manuscript of *The Outward Room* to the Simon and Schuster office.

What happened next, according to an article written by H. Allen Smith and published in the *New York World-Telegram* on Tuesday, May 4, 1937, a few days after the publication of *The Outward Room*, was this:

> At the publishing house a dozen members of the staff read it. The staff almost demanded that this book be sent to the presses. The Messrs. Simon & Schuster read it and agreed. They handed an advance copy to Sinclair Lewis. Back came

an enthusiastic letter from the Nobel Prize winner. Other writers read the advance copies, joined the chorus of cheering... By mid-February advance orders for "The Outward Room" had reached 10,000. That is somewhat more than remarkable for a first book. In March the people who run the Book-of-the-Month Club sent word that they had selected Mr. Brand's novel for distribution to their members in May...The book club selection meant an additional printing of something over 80,000 copies, all in one great fine batch. And still the regular orders flowed in. As the first of May approached the publishers announced that the first printing of "The Outward Room" would be 140,000 copies.

These remarkable circumstances prompted Simon and Schuster to include this unusual announcement on the jacket of the first edition:

A NOTE ABOUT THE PRICE OF *THE OUTWARD ROOM*

Please note that this novel is priced at $1.25 instead of $2.00. You may be interested in the reasons for this change:

Most novels are printed in editions of 3,000 copies or less. Because of advance interest in *The Outward Room* on the part of critics, fellow authors and booksellers, the first printing is 140,000.

This huge edition has made it possible for the publishers to reduce costs greatly by large purchases of cloth, paper, and other basic materials...Thus, in the case of such books as *The Outward Room*, a lower price makes it possible for tens of thousands of readers to keep a book which they wish to read and own, rather than borrow or rent it.

The book was published on May 1, 1937, the same day as William Maxwell's second novel, *They Came Like Swallows*, and the two books were featured as dual main selections of the Book-of-the-Month Club. Although Maxwell's book is set two decades earlier than Brand's, both books are written with the same empathetic tenderness, and because of this similarity, and the fact of their coincidental publishing and notice by the Book-of-the-Month Club, the books were frequently reviewed together, and compared. Ralph Thompson, in *The New York Times*, preferred Maxwell's book because it dealt with a "normal" family: "He [Maxwell] has taken an ordinary dramatic situation—one that he himself must have experienced—and developed it without pretension or affectation." Brand, on the other hand, "has chosen a theme of immense scope and implication: that of a woman's mental and moral regeneration. He cannot handle it convincingly, courageous though his attempt is." The real problem with the book, according to Thompson, is Harriet herself: "Mr. Brand's description of Harriet's unbalanced mind is hardly one that the average reader can check against his own experience...Only in the concluding pages of the novel, after months of washing John's clothes, cooking his meals and sleeping in his bed, does she assume some of the qualities of a living woman." In other words, to find Harriet sympathetic, one must be mad oneself, and her "regeneration" results from a combination of domestic servitude and sexual activity.

Although most of the reviews for both books were positive, *The Outward Room* far outsold *They Came Like Swallows*. More than half a million copies were sold, and encouraged by this commercial success, Brand quit his job at the telephone company and rented an office of his own. He set out to write a Proustian series of eight novels, of which *The Outward Room* was the first, "each of which will be an integral whole, yet dovetailing into a carefully wrought pattern of human experience." Over the following forty years, Brand did write four other novels, and published three collections of poems. Some of this work—particularly the novels *The Heroes* (1939) and *Savage Sleep* (1968), both of which refract themes and concerns of *The Outward Room*—was well reviewed, but none of his subsequent books ever received the same critical and commercial success as his first book. Reviewers were always quick to compare his later books to *The Outward Room*, and despite any merits they might posses, dismiss them. Gilbert Millstein's review of Brand's last published novel, *Some Love, Some Hunger*, concludes with a fine example of this begrudging praise: "On the whole, however, *Some Love, Some Hunger*, while worthy and honest, while devoted and true, is not the best of Millen Brand's work. It suffers from the very virtues that gave significance to *The Outward Room*...This is not a bad novel; it is not second-rate. It is simply not excellent." And so, except for a series of sensationally packaged pulp paperback editions of *The Outward Room* released in the 1950s (*"Does an insane woman have the right to love?"* *"She fled the torment of a vile place—to find savage and sudden desire in* The Outward Room"), none of his work remained in print or has been reprinted.

The Outward Room did, however, have a brief second life on the stage. *The World We Make*, a theatrical adaptation written and directed by Sidney Kingsley and starring the actress known only as "Margo," ran for eighty performances on Broadway in the fall of 1939. Brooks Atkinson championed the play with two reviews in *The New York Times*, characterizing the book as "the haunting story of a mentally unbalanced girl who escaped from an institution and healed herself by living a normal life with normal people," and concluding that the play "is brave, original, and fervent in conviction, and an ornament to our theatre." Two screen versions of the play were subsequently announced by MGM, but neither was made. The first was to star Norma Shearer and George Raft; the second ("Strangers in the Dark") was to feature Susan Peters and Gene Kelly.

Brand is perhaps best remembered, if he is remembered at all, for co-writing the Academy Award–nominated screenplay for *The Snake Pit*, a less subtle story of an institutionalized woman. Unfortunately his screenwriting career was cut short when, in 1953, because of his close association with members of the Hollywood

Ten,* he testified uncooperatively (and with Pirandellian absur-
dity) before the House Un-American Activities Committee. His
books were subsequently removed from United States Informa-
tion Service libraries in many foreign countries. Without being
able to sustain his commercial success as a writer, Brand returned
to office employment and for the following decades worked as
an editor at Crown Publishers. Toward the end of his life, he
published two books (one with photographs by George Tice
and the other a collection of poems) about the insular religious
communities of Pennsylvania. His final book, a poetic account
of his participation in the Peace March between Nagasaki and
Hiroshima in 1977, was published six months after his death
in 1980.

The origins of *The Outward Room* can be traced to Brand's
courtship of his first wife, the poet and novelist Pauline Leader.
(His second marriage, to Helen Mendelssohn, also ended in di-
vorce.) According to H. Allen Smith, in 1931 Brand read an auto-
biographical novel called *And No Birds Sang*.

> It was written by Pauline Leader and it told of the cruel and
> brutal fashion in which life had used her. When she was 12
> an illness deprived her of her hearing, and she has been deaf
> ever since. But she was a poet, with the soul and sensitivity
> of a poet. She came to New York from Vermont when she
> was 17, and lived in a windowless, three-dollar-a-week room
> in Greenwich Village. She slaved in sweatshops and washed
> dishes in restaurants, and she wrote poetry—good poetry.
> Pauline Leader's story of her life made such a deep impres-

*According to Brand's *New York Times* obituary (written by Eric Pace), "Adrian
Scott the writer-producer, and Edward Dmytryk, the director, both of whom
had been dismissed by RKO for refusing to tell a Congressional panel whether
they were members of the Communist Party, formed a corporation in 1948 to
film Mr. Brand's story of a black family moving into a white neighborhood in
Jersey City [*Albert Sears*]. Members of the Hollywood Ten, Mr. Scott and Mr.
Dmytryk went to prison for their refusal to cooperate with the committee."

sion on Millen Brand that he wrote a letter to her. They corresponded, they met and ultimately they were married.

The Outward Room is an elegantly composed novel in three distinct parts, and in each part the main character inhabits a different room and assumes a different name. The book is set in the mid-1930s; the initially unnamed heroine suffers an incapacitating depression while the country around her suffers a depression of its own. She languishes in a mental hospital, "in a wing of a building given over to the hopelessly insane." A combination of ingenuity and bravery allow her to escape from the deadening asylum and find her way to New York City, where she sets about creating a life for herself out of absolutely nothing. Like a trapped animal that chews off a limb to set itself free, the now-named Harriet pawns her only possession, her beloved dead brother's ring: "She twisted and pulled, hurting the flesh...Suddenly it came off, and like a part of herself, she saw it lying in her palm." With the five dollars she receives for the ring, she finds shelter, food, and work, and eventually is befriended by, and falls in love with, an almost ominously decent and thoughtful man. The original flap copy melodramatically states "together they face the supreme crisis of their lives."

But there is no crisis, supreme or otherwise. What Harriet and John face is life itself, the struggle and dangers and pathos and joy of the everyday, and it is Brand's disinclination to push these characters toward a more dramatically conclusive occurrence that gives *The Outward Room* its beguiling authenticity and refreshing quiet. Brand (like William Maxwell) has that rare empathetic ability to love all his characters, even those who behave meanly or badly, for he understands them too well to judge or condemn them: he looks up through them rather than down at them. And so the reader comes to feel, and fear, for the characters in a way that is almost unbearably tender. An odd glow of love permeates every aspect of this book.

Ostensibly, *The Outward Room* is a novel of recovery. It charts the (now) familiar movement from sickness to health, from darkness to light. Harriet recovers because she unneurotically takes what she is given and asks for what she wants ("I'd like a pocketbook"). Yet there is nothing formulaic or expected about this book: Brand's world is too quiveringly alive, and his writing too idiosyncratically gorgeous, to ever be predictable. The anarchic punctuation, the jangled syntax, the invented vocabulary, combined with the startlingly original way of observing the world, give Brand's sentences a startling energy and beauty. His descriptions of Depression-era New York City (the rooming houses, the elevated and subway trains, the all-night cafeterias, the sweatshops) have a stark Hopper-esque intensity and resonance. The first chapter of Part Two, which consists of a single four-page paragraph in which the homeless heroine spends the night riding the subway, is an incandescent dream of brilliant writing.

All of Brand's work is modest and sincere, two qualities that are undervalued, if not dismissed, in modern fiction. "While sensationalism flourishes around us it is hard to account for the power in literature based on ordinary things and daily life," William Stafford observed in his review of *Local Lives*, Brand's collection of poems about the Amish, Mennonite, and Quaker communities. Despite the titillating claims of the paperback reprints, there is nothing sensational about *The Outward Room*. Its power comes from its tenderness and quiet. As Brand himself observes, near the end of the book, "the evidences of winter were small, only to be seen, like the signs of spring, by the heart that feels small changes."

—PETER CAMERON

TITLES IN SERIES

J.R. ACKERLEY Hindoo Holiday
J.R. ACKERLEY My Dog Tulip
J.R. ACKERLEY My Father and Myself
J.R. ACKERLEY We Think the World of You
HENRY ADAMS The Jeffersonian Transformation
CÉLESTE ALBARET Monsieur Proust
DANTE ALIGHIERI The Inferno
DANTE ALIGHIERI The New Life
WILLIAM ATTAWAY Blood on the Forge
W.H. AUDEN (EDITOR) The Living Thoughts of Kierkegaard
W.H. AUDEN W.H. Auden's Book of Light Verse
ERICH AUERBACH Dante: Poet of the Secular World
DOROTHY BAKER Cassandra at the Wedding
J.A. BAKER The Peregrine
HONORÉ DE BALZAC The Unknown Masterpiece *and* Gambara
MAX BEERBOHM Seven Men
STEPHEN BENATAR Wish Her Safe at Home
FRANS G. BENGTSSON The Long Ships
ALEXANDER BERKMAN Prison Memoirs of an Anarchist
GEORGES BERNANOS Mouchette
ADOLFO BIOY CASARES Asleep in the Sun
ADOLFO BIOY CASARES The Invention of Morel
CAROLINE BLACKWOOD Corrigan
CAROLINE BLACKWOOD Great Granny Webster
NICOLAS BOUVIER The Way of the World
MALCOLM BRALY On the Yard
MILLEN BRAND The Outward Room
JOHN HORNE BURNS The Gallery
ROBERT BURTON The Anatomy of Melancholy
CAMARA LAYE The Radiance of the King
GIROLAMO CARDANO The Book of My Life
DON CARPENTER Hard Rain Falling
J.L. CARR A Month in the Country
BLAISE CENDRARS Moravagine
EILEEN CHANG Love in a Fallen City
UPAMANYU CHATTERJEE English, August: An Indian Story
NIRAD C. CHAUDHURI The Autobiography of an Unknown Indian
ANTON CHEKHOV Peasants and Other Stories
RICHARD COBB Paris and Elsewhere
COLETTE The Pure and the Impure
JOHN COLLIER Fancies and Goodnights
CARLO COLLODI The Adventures of Pinocchio
IVY COMPTON-BURNETT A House and Its Head
IVY COMPTON-BURNETT Manservant and Maidservant
BARBARA COMYNS The Vet's Daughter
EVAN S. CONNELL The Diary of a Rapist
ALBERT COSSERY The Jokers
HAROLD CRUSE The Crisis of the Negro Intellectual
ASTOLPHE DE CUSTINE Letters from Russia

For a complete list of titles, visit www.nyrb.com or write to:
Catalog Requests, NYRB, 435 Hudson Street, New York, NY 10014

ELIZABETH HARDWICK Sleepless Nights
L.P. HARTLEY Eustace and Hilda: A Trilogy
L.P. HARTLEY The Go-Between
NATHANIEL HAWTHORNE Twenty Days with Julian & Little Bunny by Papa
GILBERT HIGHET Poets in a Landscape
JANET HOBHOUSE The Furies
HUGO VON HOFMANNSTHAL The Lord Chandos Letter
JAMES HOGG The Private Memoirs and Confessions of a Justified Sinner
RICHARD HOLMES Shelley: The Pursuit
ALISTAIR HORNE A Savage War of Peace: Algeria 1954–1962
WILLIAM DEAN HOWELLS Indian Summer
RICHARD HUGHES A High Wind in Jamaica
RICHARD HUGHES In Hazard
RICHARD HUGHES The Fox in the Attic (The Human Predicament, Vol. 1)
RICHARD HUGHES The Wooden Shepherdess (The Human Predicament, Vol. 2)
MAUDE HUTCHINS Victorine
HENRY JAMES The Ivory Tower
HENRY JAMES The New York Stories of Henry James
HENRY JAMES The Other House
HENRY JAMES The Outcry
TOVE JANSSON The Summer Book
TOVE JANSSON The True Deceiver
RANDALL JARRELL (EDITOR) Randall Jarrell's Book of Stories
DAVID JONES In Parenthesis
ERNST JÜNGER The Glass Bees
HELEN KELLER The World I Live In
FRIGYES KARINTHY A Journey Round My Skull
YASHAR KEMAL Memed, My Hawk
YASHAR KEMAL They Burn the Thistles
MURRAY KEMPTON Part of Our Time: Some Ruins and Monuments of the Thirties
DAVID KIDD Peking Story
ROBERT KIRK The Secret Commonwealth of Elves, Fauns, and Fairies
ARUN KOLATKAR Jejuri
DEZSŐ KOSZTOLÁNYI Skylark
TÉTÉ-MICHEL KPOMASSIE An African in Greenland
GYULA KRÚDY Sunflower
SIGIZMUND KRZHIZHANOVSKY Memories of the Future
PATRICK LEIGH FERMOR Between the Woods and the Water
PATRICK LEIGH FERMOR Mani: Travels in the Southern Peloponnese
PATRICK LEIGH FERMOR Roumeli: Travels in Northern Greece
PATRICK LEIGH FERMOR A Time of Gifts
PATRICK LEIGH FERMOR A Time to Keep Silence
D.B. WYNDHAM LEWIS AND CHARLES LEE (EDITORS) The Stuffed Owl
GEORG CHRISTOPH LICHTENBERG The Waste Books
JAKOV LIND Soul of Wood and Other Stories
H.P. LOVECRAFT AND OTHERS The Colour Out of Space
ROSE MACAULAY The Towers of Trebizond
NORMAN MAILER Miami and the Siege of Chicago
JANET MALCOLM In the Freud Archives
OSIP MANDELSTAM The Selected Poems of Osip Mandelstam
OLIVIA MANNING Fortunes of War: The Balkan Trilogy
OLIVIA MANNING School for Love